A NOVEL BASED ON THE LIFE OF
SCIPIO AFRICANUS

RIDE INTO THE SUN

Patric Verrone

THE MENTORIS PROJECT

Ride Into the Sun is a work of fiction. Some incidents, dialogue, and characters are products of the author's imagination and are not to be construed as real. Where real-life historical figures appear, the situations, incidents, and dialogue concerning those persons are based on or inspired by actual events. In all other respects, any resemblance to actual persons, living or dead, events, or locales is entirely coincidental.

Barbera Foundation, Inc.
P.O. Box 1019
Temple City, CA 91780

Copyright © 2018 Barbera Foundation, Inc.
Cover photo: Classic Image / Alamy Stock Photo
Cover design: Suzanne Turpin

More information at www.mentorisproject.org

ISBN: 978-1-947431-19-5

Library of Congress Control Number: 2018957764

All net proceeds from the sale of this book will be donated to Barbera Foundation, Inc. whose mission is to support educational initiatives that foster an appreciation of history and culture to encourage and inspire young people to create a stronger future.

The Mentoris Project is a series of novels and biographies about the lives of great men and women who have changed history through their contributions as scientists, inventors, explorers, thinkers, and creators. The Barbera Foundation sponsors this series in the hope that, like a mentor, each book will inspire the reader to discover how she or he can make a positive contribution to society.

Contents

Foreword

First and foremost, Mentor was a person. We tend to think of the word *mentor* as a noun (a mentor) or a verb (to mentor), but there is a very human dimension embedded in the term. Mentor appears in Homer's *Odyssey* as the old friend entrusted to care for Odysseus's household and his son Telemachus during the Trojan War. When years pass and Telemachus sets out to search for his missing father, the goddess Athena assumes the form of Mentor to accompany him. The human being welcomes a human form for counsel. From its very origins, becoming a mentor is a transcendent act; it carries with it something of the holy.

The Mentoris Project sets out on an Athena-like mission: We hope the books that form this series will be an inspiration to all those who are seekers, to those of the twenty-first century who are on their own odysseys, trying to find enduring principles that will guide them to a spiritual home. The stories that comprise the series are all deeply human. These books dramatize the lives of great men and women whose stories bridge the ancient and the modern, taking many forms, just as Athena did, but always holding up a light for those living today.

Whether in novel form or traditional biography, these books plumb the individual characters of our heroes' journeys.

The power of storytelling has always been to envelop the reader in a vivid and continuous dream, and to forge a link with the subject. Our goal is for that link to guide the reader home with a new inspiration.

What is a mentor? A guide, a moral compass, an inspiration. A friend who points you toward true north. We hope that the Mentoris Project will become that friend, and it will help us all transcend our daily lives with something that can only be called holy.

—Robert J. Barbera, President, Barbera Foundation
—Ken LaZebnik, Founding Editor, The Mentoris Project

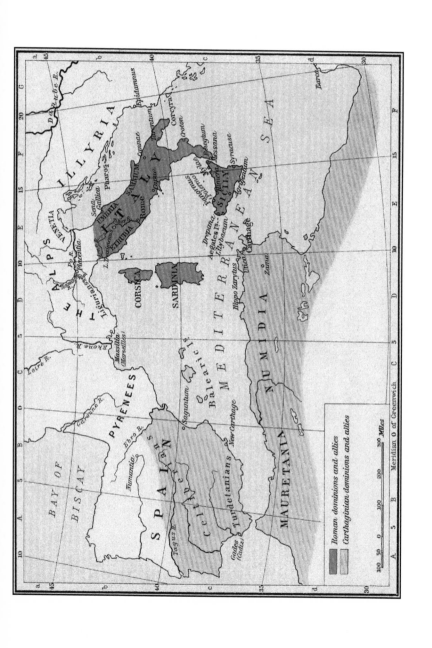

Chapter One

Laelius remembered standing valiantly at the bow of an immense ship at the head of the Roman fleet in the center of the marketplace. He recalled holding his sword outstretched before him as he faced down Hamilcar Barca, commander of the Carthaginian forces.

"Your fleet is no match against the power of the Roman Republic," Laelius said.

"Rome is a state of cowards. Do your worst!" Hamilcar Barca said just before Laelius gave the command to pursue the Carthaginian fleet around the island of Sicily.

The turbulent Mediterranean frothed beneath their ships. The wind whipped through Laelius's hair. Soon, Laelius heroically leapt from his ship onto Hamilcar Barca's, and steel met steel. The two great men battled until their swords were thrown aside and they wrestled on the deck of the ship. Then, Laelius remembered knocking into the olive oil seller's booth and nearly toppling a row of carafes. Their imaginary battle was shattered by the merchant, who chased them out of the marketplace.

Laelius thought back on his childhood fondly, when he and the other boys would reenact battles from the First War against Carthage. They would terrorize the merchants and patrons of the Roman market with their overactive imaginations. Laelius's favorite was the Battle of the Aegates Islands, the battle that concluded the war and ousted the Carthaginians from Sicily. Everyone always fought over who would play the Romans and who would have to play Hamilcar Barca. Sometimes if the boy playing Hamilcar was particularly strong, he would knock the Romans over and rewrite history by claiming victory for the Carthaginians. If this happened, the other boys would pile onto him and reassert Rome's superiority.

As Laelius grew older, he realized that the reality was much grimmer than his play. The Rome into which Laelius had been born was a Rome of war. Rome had established itself as a superpower in Europe, rising above the smaller Italian kingdoms that populated the north, south, and Sardinian islands off the coast. No other power in Italy would dare challenge the massive Republic's control over the region. However, Carthage was no longer just a struggling African principality across the sea. Every day, news came of Carthage's allies landing in Iberia or their occupation of the Italian islands in the south. What history might consider peacetime after the end of the First Punic War was filled with paranoia, fear-mongering, and confusion. Not long after peace was negotiated, rumors arose of Hamilcar Barca's son, the great and enterprising Hannibal, building another army to avenge his family's name. The First War had drained Rome of its resources and its people's pride, and yet somehow it seemed to have made Rome's enemies across the Mediterranean only stronger. As Laelius and his friends transformed Rome's battles into games, the rest of the city held its breath, fearing that Carthage would take its revenge.

Then, that fateful summer came. Word began to trickle in of Hannibal crossing the Alps into Italy. What was first dismissed as disparate drops of rumor and conjecture had, by the end of that summer, risen into a tumultuous ocean of truth. Laelius could remember the days when people began to truly understand what Hannibal had done. They were angry and scared. They wanted to fight or flee into the sea or plead the gods for mercy. But even in all that desperation, that summer was quiet. The birds didn't sing, the bees didn't hum, and the grass was always still. Yet, the fragile peace had finally broken and, as Rome scrambled to gather the pieces, Hannibal crossed onto Italian soil.

The Roman Senate was in utter disarray. They were a long way from recovering after the First War, and Hannibal's sudden descent into Italy had left them scrambling to sort out who would lead the charge and who would lead the Republic. Many of Rome's most prominent families had lost men in the First War, so the senate was put in the position of redeploying the statesmen who had survived. A large portion of these men were injured or exhausted and in no hurry to return to the battlefield. The senate erupted in bickering with consuls accusing one another of nepotism, cowardice, and traitorous activity during the First War. It was in this maelstrom that Publius the Elder and his brother Gnaeus decided that action had to be taken. Both well-respected men from the prominent Scipio family and both heroes of the First War, they took it upon themselves to form legions in northern Italy as the first line of defense against Hannibal should he march on Rome.

Many of the other boys whom Laelius had played with in

the marketplace were excited to join the Scipio brothers' army when they turned eighteen, sometimes younger. They all warmly remembered the war games they'd played and jumped at the chance to become real heroes themselves. Laelius, who'd left his childhood days of play to help his father tend to the horses on their farm, began to dream more and more of the valiant deeds, heroic victories, energetic sparring, and spectacular deaths he and his comrades had performed. Just a few weeks after the news of Hannibal's crossing into Italy had been solidified into Roman minds as fact, Laelius was on his way to join Publius the Elder's legion at Pisa.

The journey felt strange to Laelius. He had never ventured more than a few miles beyond the city, and everything was new to his senses. Even the words sounded different in the mouths of the locals. Laelius had grown up as an only child with his mother and father. He kept to himself during most of his journey. He could not understand why the other boys became so delighted in being worked up by rumors about Hannibal's army: tales of great Numidian cavalrymen who were such brilliant horsemen it was as if they became centaurs in the frenzy of the battlefield; savage warriors from Gaul with skin like marble stone; and great beasts the size of buildings, called elephants, that Hannibal had brought with him over the mountains.

Laelius's father was a horseman and Laelius had grown up caring for and riding horses all his life. Because of this, he was accepted into the legion's modest cavalry. The other cavalrymen were the sons of noblemen or statesmen who had learned horse riding as a part of their illustrious educations. Most of them were uninterested in interacting with Laelius, who was decidedly of a lower class. There was, however, one fellow horseman who took an interest in the quiet horse breeder's son.

The wind had picked up toward the end of summer and the breeze was pleasantly cooling. Laelius was attending to a stallion he had taken a liking to, nicknamed Narcissus for the long drinks that he took, making it seem as if he were engrossed in his reflection.

Another cavalryman rode up beside him. Laelius recognized him as the commander's son Scipio. Though not terribly handsome, he had a strong soldier's build and the high forehead attributed to wise men, as well as a clever twinkle in his eye. Aside from these, his features were distinctly Roman.

"Ride with me?" he asked.

"Where to?" Laelius replied.

"Into the sun. If we catch it, Apollo will have to give us two of the stallions from his chariot."

Laelius mounted his horse, and the two of them took off westward. They rode as far as they could, but as the sun began to set, the chances of catching up to Apollo's chariot fell with it. They slowed to catch their breath.

"I see you alone most of the time," said the commander's son. "Why is that?"

"I don't think I have much in common with anybody else in the legion."

"We're all Roman." He turned and started back toward the camp.

Laelius urged Narcissus forward and rode beside Scipio. From that point on, the two men became inseparable.

Life in the camp was a mixture of gradual preparation for an attack and cautious relaxation. Word of the army's movements reached the camp through multiple Roman allies and spies throughout northern Italy, but no one could quite make sense of what Hannibal's plan was. The senate feared he would eventually take his army down to Rome and it was the job of Scipio's legion to make sure he didn't get that far. When they weren't preparing for an altercation with Hannibal, the soldiers played games. Those in the cavalry raced or dared one another to jump and dodge obstacles on their horses. It soon became clear to everyone in the legion that Scipio and Laelius were the most accomplished riders at the Pisa camp.

On a day when the lingering summer heat numbed the limbs into extreme lethargy, Scipio, Laelius, and a few other soldiers gathered by the bank of the Rhône. The trees had just begun turning from green into brown and red. Some of the leaves had fallen in swirling circles in the river, green beside red, two seasons rushing southward. Laelius was basking on a rock perched above a deep, lazy pool in which the stones had caught the river. Scipio was speaking to a few of the other soldiers behind him. As Laelius watched the leaves dancing in the water, he was surprised to find them speedily racing toward him. He broke through the water headfirst and quickly resurfaced to see who had pushed him.

Scipio looked down at him, a satisfied smirk splashing across his face. Laelius tried climbing the rock to pull his friend down with him. The other men laughed and some even tried pushing Laelius back into the water. Laelius finally gave up on climbing back up the rock and instead swam to the shore. He quietly crouched in the grass, listening to the muffled, anticipatory chuckles from the other men. Laelius leapt from the grass and began to wrestle Scipio along the bank. He was older than Scipio and physically stronger and, after a brief tussle, he was able to lurch both of them into the river. The sound of Scipio and Laelius splashing and the other men cheering and booing covered the slow approach of horse hooves.

One of the men gave out a cry. Scipio and Laelius resurfaced just as a small band of Numidian horseman burst into the clearing. They wore golden lioness hides across their shoulders and poised slings and javelins above their heads. After a chilling heartbeat of recognition, the leader of the group charged right at Scipio and Laelius. The two Roman boys rolled out of the way and into the tall grass. Their comrades quickly gathered their shields and spears. The band of Numidians was small, but still outnumbered the soldiers slightly—and besides, they had horses and the element of surprise on their side. Scipio leapt out of the grass and grabbed his shield, turning just in time for the large iron circle to catch a flying javelin that would have gouged his thigh. Scipio tossed a spear to Laelius, who, with a burst of adrenaline even he did not know he was capable of, launched the spear further than he ever had and hit one of the Numidian's horses in its back leg. The rider dropped his sling and toppled into the river.

Laelius dove into the water to grab the weapon. He heard Scipio shout behind him. He was wielding a large rock and gesturing to the sling. Laelius grabbed it before it floated downstream and tossed it to him. Scipio placed the rock in the sling, swung it above his head, and lobbed it at the rider who had charged at Laelius and Scipio, hitting him between the eyes with a gut-wrenching crack! The man rolled off his horse and into another rider. Their leader unconscious, the Numidian band quickly retreated. All the Roman men were accounted for, and helped a comrade who had been struck in the shoulder by a javelin to walk back to camp.

~

Back at the military base in Pisa, Scipio headed straight to his father's tent. He insisted that Laelius accompany him to vouch for the events at the Rhône. When the two boys entered Publius the Elder's tent, they found him speaking with two of his head generals, Caius and Sempronius. Scipio described the Numidian attack at the river, and Publius the Elder immediately went to a large map of the region laid out on a wooden table. Scipio's father flanked the sides of the map with the palms of his hands, giving him leverage to lean against the table and look directly down onto the inked depictions of the Rhône, the Ticinus, and Pisa.

"What did the riders look like?" Publius the Elder inquired once his son finished his account.

"They wore lioness skins instead of shields," Laelius piped up.

Publius the Elder gravely studied his map. "They are Hannibal's men, then. We've received reports from northern allies of a similar group of Numidian cavalrymen marching with Hannibal's main force. They were likely sent before the army to scout the area and they'll have told Hannibal where he found you. His camp must be close." He turned to one of his generals. "Caius, ready a group of our best cavalrymen and velites to form a reconnaissance mission. We will march northward and westward in a wide sweep toward the mountains and gather whatever intel on Hannibal's movements and whereabouts we can. It will be impossible for him to evade us or travel any further south, and once we return, we will assess our viability of attack."

"Laelius and I will go," Scipio volunteered.

"You have helped us enough already," his father assured him. "You said that you wanted the best cavalrymen on this mission. Laelius and I are the most experienced riders in this entire legion."

"He is right, sir," Caius conceded. "These young men have bested their peers and soldiers much older in most of the riding games."

"He is too young. Son, you are only just eighteen and will be of much more help here at the camp—"

"Doing what? Playing more games?" Scipio interrupted.

The tent was saturated with tension that ran deeper than military insubordination: father versus son. Scipio's defiant, youthful expression was mirrored in his father's older but equally challenging face.

After a few heartbeats, Scipio softened and spoke. "I came here with you to fight on behalf of Rome. I would be more helpful with you on this mission."

Though Publius the Elder's expression did not shift, something in the hazel eyes he had passed down to his firstborn softened along with Scipio. "You will be included on the mission, but you will also be accompanied by a protectorate of cavalrymen to assure your safety."

"As long as Laelius can be included in my protectorate," Scipio immediately countered.

It shocked Laelius how readily Scipio demanded concessions from his father and commanding officer.

Publius the Elder nodded. "Ready your things, then. You two are dismissed." He gestured for Sempronius to join him at the table and the two immediately began poring over the map.

Laelius turned to leave the tent, but Scipio did not move. He hesitated, as if waiting for something.

Publius the Elder glanced up from the map. "I said 'dismissed,' boys."

Scipio turned on his heel and exited the tent with Laelius in pursuit.

"Scipio, what was that?"

"I don't know what you mean." Scipio refused to turn his head and meet Laelius's eyes.

"I mean back there, with your father—"

"That was me getting you a better position. You don't think the commander would have included you in this mission if it weren't for me, do you? You might say 'thank you,'" Scipio snapped.

A poisonous pang of aggression flared up inside of Laelius at his friend's arrogance, but died as quickly as it had come. Laelius had killed his temper at the age of twelve when a fistfight he had won against a consul's son had resulted in his own father beating him. How would he fare if he struck the son of his legion's commander?

Instead, Laelius remarked, "I only mean it was pretty brave of you to speak to your father with so much authority."

Scipio shrugged and mumbled something about going to pack his things. Laelius watched his friend disappear amid the other soldiers. The enemy of Temper was Patience, which Laelius had learned years ago. Perhaps in time his friend's distress would become clear to him.

Marching north, Laelius saw the full extent of autumn's Midas touch on the country. All that was green a few miles south had been transformed into yellows and golds. The more north he went, the faster time seemed to race by. The reconnaissance force consisted of about four hundred velites, Rome's light infantrymen, and twenty-five hundred cavalrymen, both Roman and

Celtic mercenaries. Scipio's protectorate was a small subset of the cavalry, handpicked by Publius the Elder and led by Laelius at Scipio's request. Laelius could tell that Scipio was not thrilled to be surrounded by a garrison of his fellow cavalrymen to ensure his safety at all times, but he had at least made it onto the mission. They had almost reached the Ticinus River, but still they hadn't caught a glimpse of the Carthaginian army.

The sun was high in the sky as Publius the Elder and his modest army approached the Ticinus. Scipio and Laelius were debating whether Narcissus was an appropriate nickname for his horse, given that she was female, when both heard a great gust of wind and saw a horse further up rear back. A spear was lodged in the grass in front of the horse's hooves. Out of the shadows, like wood nymphs emerging from their arboreal forms, a group of Carthaginian spearmen appeared. Soon, thousands of soldiers emerged by the banks of the river: Carthaginian infantrymen, Numidian cavalry, Celtic mercenaries, and Iberian warriors. They had found Hannibal's army.

A Carthaginian general shouted across the field to Publius the Elder, a saccharine grin on his face. "We have come seeking but one thing, something that our great Hannibal is yet to have received: the dripping, bloody head of a Roman consul." The general let out a bloodcurdling screech and the Carthaginian forces descended upon the Romans.

Laelius and Scipio's protectorate immediately bolstered themselves despite Scipio's protests.

"Get out of the way and let me fight!" Scipio yelled.

A spear whizzed over Laelius's head just as a Numidian rider sped at him from the left. Laelius swung his sword and felt it hit the rider's shield. He found himself facing another rider, who gave a loud shout and charged at him headlong. Laelius swerved

Narcissus to the rider's left and swung his sword again. This time he hit flesh, but the rider was lost in the chaos of the battle.

"Father!"

Laelius heard Scipio's cry and turned to see that a number of spearmen had encircled Publius the Elder. The commander was fighting valiantly, but had been injured. Blood covered his face and arms, and he fell to one knee every time he swung his sword.

"Help the commander!" Scipio looked around frantically for his protectorate, but it had dwindled to three cavalry. "Don't any of you hear me?"

"We're meant to protect you!" one of the protectorate shouted. "Your father told us—"

"My father, your commander, is going to die!" Scipio looked at Laelius pleadingly.

Laelius nodded, raised his sword, and announced a charge. Scipio, Laelius, and what was left of the protectorate charged at the spearmen. Laelius was immediately locked in combat with one who used his small spear as a lance and kept trying to stab at Laelius's horse. But Laelius was too quick and nimble on horseback and struck the spearman down.

After felling the Carthaginian soldier, Laelius looked up at a sight that would later cause him to wonder whether it had been a dream. Scipio had jumped off his horse and was steadily cutting down experienced enemy soldiers to reach his father. Publius the Elder had fallen with barely enough strength to hold up his shield to defend himself against the enemy's blows. But Scipio, with his cinnamon curls, youthful limbs, and powerful yet graceful gait, looked like a hero of myth. Never before had Laelius seen a man with such yearning flames in his eyes. Those flames powered an engine within Scipio that drove him forward until the boy stood over his father. The young man helped his injured, half-conscious father onto his horse before mounting it himself. Then, with the same power that drove him through layer after layer of Carthaginian warriors, Scipio sped his horse off the battlefield and out of harm's way. He was out of sight in seconds.

After the battle had ended, Laelius and the rest of the protectorate rejoined General Sempronius's troops. They returned with them to Pisa, where Laelius met Scipio again. Scipio had ridden all day and through the night to get his father to the base's medic. Though he had lost some blood and been badly bruised, his father would be all right the medic said. Scipio stood outside of the infirmary tent, absentmindedly stroking his exhausted steed.

Laelius approached Scipio. Unsure of what to say, he began to pet the animal's muzzle, which made Scipio smile, even if just out of the corners of his lips.

"How did we fare?" Laelius asked.

"Not well. We lost a lot of men—at least half of the reconnaissance mission. Those who were left retreated. Hannibal's forces outnumbered us too much."

"Did you see him?"

"Who?"

"Hannibal."

A red streak of hatred flashed in Scipio's eyes. "No."

"Neither did I."

Hannibal's failure to make an appearance seemed to frustrate Scipio even more. He no longer felt a vague hatred for the general threatening Rome, but was personally offended that Hannibal did not fight his own battles. Laelius put his hand on Scipio's shoulder.

Suddenly, a large mob of soldiers approached Scipio. He

straightened his back in order to look more soldierly despite his own exhaustion. The crowd continued to grow until almost the entire camp was assembled. Unsure of the mob's intentions, Laelius touched the hilt of his sword.

General Sempronius stepped forward. "Publius Cornelius Scipio, son of Publius the Elder, the bravery and gravitas that you exemplified in defending and rescuing our commander are like none I have ever seen in years of combat. By Jupiter, all of Rome will know the feats you have performed in the name of the Republic."

The entire crowd erupted into a thunderous applause that made the ground beneath their feet shake. Scipio's career had begun.

Chapter Two

HOME—217 B.C.

The entire city of Rome was buzzing with the news of Scipio's heroic rescue. While some cynical or jealous statesmen asserted that the story was an exaggeration or a nepotistic ploy by Publius the Elder to better his son's position, most of the people of Rome began to view Scipio as a glowing ray of hope against the ever-darkening threat of Hannibal. As autumn shifted to winter, Scipio and his father returned to Rome to help Publius the Elder's recovery. Scipio insisted that Laelius come with them.

The Scipio family was one of the oldest and most prominent families in Rome. The family's ancestors had been instrumental in the founding of the Republic and the patriarchs of the family had proven themselves again and again throughout Rome's history. The halls of the Roman Senate echoed the triumphant pontifications of Scipio's ancestors. Three generations of his lineage were renowned as heroes of the First War.

Though Laelius had gazed at the houses of noble families up on the hills just outside the city, he could never have imagined the splendor that lay within their walls. Some of the interior walls were painstakingly painted to resemble marble and were decorated with cornices and reliefs of busts of Scipio's ancestors that protruded from the wall and seemed to follow you with their eyes. Others were painted with murals that mimicked looking out from the inside of a large forum. In the foreground, the painter had replicated realistic columns that obscured a breathtaking view of the city. Walking through the halls of Villa Scipio, Laelius looked out onto painted scenes of the Roman marketplace, architects building the Coliseum, chariot races in motion, and the climax of a popular Roman tragedy. The most remarkable of all was an enormous rendering of the construction of the Roman Senate chambers, a symbol of the victory of the Republic over the oppressive kings that had once held dominion over the city. Colorful tiles of vibrant red, sandy yellow, and the deepest ocean blue, some with gold accents, were inlaid in the floor in intricate mosaics. Laelius walked above brilliant recreations of Romulus and Remus being raised by their wolf mother, Hercules defeating the Nemean Lion, and glorious battles of the First War that sparkled with newness.

The atrium just beyond the entrance of the house was a wide-open space filled with foliage, marble benches, and small bronze bird feeders. It connected all of the other rooms of the house. In the center stood a statue of Vesta, goddess of home and hearth, the size of an actual Roman woman. Her face had been carved to resemble a great-grandmother of Scipio's. She welcomed visitors into her family's home, while at her feet a small stone fountain burbled. When it rained, the water would pour down her arms and feed the fountain, causing it to overflow into small rivers that snaked across the atrium and collected underground.

The garden in Villa Scipio was particularly renowned for exotic vines and blossoms that Publius the Elder and Gnaeus had brought back from their military campaigns. While veterans of the First War had brought back gems, golden jewelry, animal hides, and other such spoils of war to decorate their homesteads, Publius the Elder and his brother had included in their souvenirs seeds from across the Mediterranean. With the caring oversight of Scipio's mother, this foreign flora had bloomed extravagantly and filled the entire house with fragrances found nowhere else in the city. Olive trees intermingled with passion fruit. Greek orchids grew beside Spanish bluebells. The garden was a fantastic sight that few Roman citizens were lucky enough to behold.

Laelius was one of those lucky few. He and Scipio spent much of their winter days sparring and riding horseback on the grounds of Villa Scipio. Meanwhile, outside the home, Scipio's fame grew. When the two friends attended a chariot race or gladiator games at the Coliseum, they would catch glimpses of Roman civilians looking their way and whispering excitedly. Crowds formed around them at the forum or the market, praising Scipio's bravery. The attention overwhelmed Laelius and made his heart flutter and his stomach fall, but Scipio received his admirers with grace and dignity.

While the two friends delighted in Scipio's new celebrity, Scipio's father and uncle were busy outlining their next move against Hannibal. Having fully recovered, Publius the Elder spent weeks appealing to the senate for more men and provisions. They had not anticipated the size of the force that Hannibal had successfully marched over the mountains, and any chance of defeating him lay in increasing Rome's defense. The senate, still disorganized, chaotic, and corrupt, did little to assist Publius the Elder. Scipio and Laelius would return to Villa Scipio in the evening and, more often than not, find Publius the Elder and Gnaeus strategizing.

Though Laelius began to learn more about his friend the more time he spent in Villa Scipio with his family, the biggest revelation came in meeting Aemelia. Aemelia Paulla was the daughter of another of Rome's prominent families. The Paulluses and Scipios had been close allies since the founding of the city. Though her lineage was ancient, Aemelia was nothing if not a modern lady.

Laelius and Scipio were returning home from one of the many baths in the city when, upon entering the atrium, Scipio stopped and blanched. In the garden, seated beside Vesta's fountain, was an arrestingly beautiful girl. She had high, regal cheekbones, but round cheeks that showed her youthfulness. Her dark, almost black hair was tied into a ponytail that flowed over her shoulder.

Aemelia strode up to the frozen Scipio and said, "I'd heard talk that you were back home, but I couldn't imagine my friend Publius Cornelius Scipio returning without sending word to me."

Scipio rediscovered his voice and squeaked, "I'm sorry, I have been preoccupied with my friend."

Aemelia turned to Laelius. "So, you're to blame." She flashed him a coy smirk and extended her hand and introduced herself as Aemelia. Laelius kissed her knuckles and introduced himself to her.

She stepped back and regarded Laelius. "A word of advice from an old friend of Cornelius, Laelius: Don't forgive him so easily. He doesn't make many mistakes, so you have to relish in the rarity."

Dinner at Villa Scipio was an event every evening. As the

sun dipped below the hills, the servants presented mouthwatering banquets of bread, cheese, fish, and olive oil. Fruits from the garden were served in great metal bowls, and sometimes a lyre player was invited to accompany the meal. Dinnertime was also a battle, for Publius the Elder was not only a general on the field, but also in his home, especially with his eldest son.

"The *corona civica*," Publius the Elder said, emphatically waving a half-eaten crust of bread, "is Rome's highest military decoration for bravery. What you did on the banks of the Ticinus was the bravest act that most of those soldiers have seen—will *ever* see. How can you refuse such a reward?"

"The action was one that awarded itself," Scipio said frankly, dunking his own crust into an amber pool of oil. "Having you alive at this table is enough of a reward, father." Scipio met his father's eyes.

Publius the Elder nodded, then turned to Laelius. "Perhaps you can convince my son, since it is evident that I am not getting through."

Laelius laughed, but saw Scipio sigh softly out of the corner of his eye.

After dinner, Laelius was walking along the halls of the atrium when he noticed Scipio sitting in a corner of the garden. It had rained that morning and raindrops still fell from some of the foliage. The night sky was clear and the air smelled fresh. Laelius sat beside his friend.

"Why don't you try for the corona civica? The senators might say you're too young, but anybody from the legion who saw what you did would defend you."

Scipio stared at a large, indigo-blue blossom. "I know this garden best in winter. When I was growing up, this house felt empty during the springs and summers when my father and uncle would be away on a campaign. I could run throughout the entire house and nobody would protest—not Mother, not the cooks or gardeners or painters. But during the winter, Father and Uncle would be strategizing or conversing with generals in the triclinium or tablinum. I grew up surrounded by talk of foreign offensives in lands I had never seen, of soldierly conduct, integrity, and gravitas, and tales of heroes. I would hear the women or the other boys in the forum talking about Father's glorious achievements on behalf of the Republic. I didn't believe that he performed any of those heroic acts because of some prize. I don't believe one should act for those reasons."

Scipio's head dropped. The tips of his curls sparked auburn against the olive oil–burning lamps. "My father wants me to be rewarded for my actions because of lesser men, but I act because of those greater than myself."

"You mean like your father?"

Scipio sighed. "He wants this for me, but he wants it more for our family. He wants it for himself. The greatest reward I could ever receive is his thanks."

A chilling wind blew past and the two boys shivered. They decided to warm themselves by the closest brazier. Watching the flames dance between his fingers, Laelius felt closer to Scipio than he had to any other person.

"When the First War broke out," Laelius said, "the senate asked my father to supply some of our horses for the cause. He was happy to give them up and excited to fight for the Republic. But a few days before he was planning to leave with the other men to become soldiers, a horse kicked him in his right leg. My mother urged the rest of the family to bring him to a doctor in the city, but they all said it would be the end of him. My father recovered, but he was rendered lame and unable to fight in the war. I remember feeling so much shame. I was the only boy whose father was not fighting. I remember thinking to myself that I had to be careful, that I couldn't risk the same thing happening to our entire family or I would pay for it. I have done the legwork for both my father and me since his accident. I have always been as careful as I could manage. I could not risk an accident. I decided that whenever I became old enough, I would fight for both of us. Every day I am proving my family's worth, trying to beat back the shame I felt as a child."

Scipio grabbed Laelius's shoulders and looked him in the eye. The low burn of the brazier reflected on his serious expression. "Laelius," he said, "if ever there comes a time, I will do everything in my power to help you restore honor and glory on your family. I swear by Jupiter."

Laelius had heard of prophesies witnessed by oracles in flames, but had paid little attention to those myths. Now, however, those legends flooded back to him as he stared into his friend's face lit by the bronze brazier. He saw Scipio in quite a different light—not the low orange of oil lamps, but the blinding white of a summer sun. Unlike at the banks of the Ticinus, he did not see Scipio as a youthful demigod, but as an older iteration of himself. Scipio was a great leader: respected, revered, and glorious. If Laelius could depend on one man to help him redeem his family, it was Scipio.

As the winter thawed gradually into spring, Publius the Elder and Gnaeus prepared to return to the field. Their appeals to the senate had finally yielded some progress. The senate would deploy four new legions northward to prevent Hannibal from coming any further south, as well as make up the loss that Publius the Elder had suffered at the Ticinus. Gnaeus would return to Spain to continue fighting off Hannibal's generals Hasdrubal and Hanno, while Publius the Elder would return to Pisa with Scipio and Laelius to pursue Hannibal's forces where they had left them in the autumn. General Flaminius, a renowned leader from the First War, would lead a separate campaign in Tuscany to solidify Rome's defenses eastward.

The day before they were set to depart with the rest of the army, Laelius discovered Scipio whispering with Aemelia fervently in the garden. Scipio held her hand tightly in his. Aemelia was teary-eyed, though she had a smile across her lips. Laelius could not discern whether her tears meant sadness or happiness, and in the end he understood that it must have been a bittersweet mixture of the two. Together, Scipio and Aemelia filled the garden with intimate warmth that almost made Laelius forget that winter was only just departing.

Later, after Aemelia had returned home, Laelius found his friend staring up into the face of Vesta. He approached her as well.

"You love her," Laelius said.

Scipio nodded. The fact was plain enough. "I have promised to marry her if I return from this campaign." The bitter morbidity of the statement made Scipio scowl.

"Well, then, a celebration is in order," Laelius said, clapping Scipio on the back hard, knocking the morose air out of him.

Scipio was so startled that he couldn't help but laugh.

That evening, the banquet tasted of apprehension and anticipation. Recent news from the senate had only created further anxiety at Scipio's table.

"Fabius Maximus is a dictator," Publius the Elder asserted.

"It is troubling how readily the other senators elected him as a leader," Gnaeus commented, biting into a hunk of cheese. "He

22

has far less experience leading in wartime than many of them. I don't understand it."

"They are afraid," Publius the Elder said. "Winter is thawing and for months the only news we've heard is that Hannibal has advanced. Defeat after defeat, and so whom do they put in charge? A delayer. Fabius Maximus's only true talent is his ability to suspend making deliberate decisions. They don't know what to do, so they would rather follow someone who does nothing than someone who takes the wrong action."

"You would rather they have elected someone more decisive?" Scipio asked.

Publius the Elder looked across the table at his son. "I would rather they had maintained the integrity of the Republic. Your forefathers fought against the rule of a monarch because they believed that no one man should be given power over all. They were tired of living under tyrants. They believed that the people deserved to elect their own leaders. Whatever actions we take now, we must remember those beliefs for which the men who battled for our Republic fought."

Scipio had straightened up in his chair. He nodded solemnly at his father's words, absorbing them into the depths of his heart and mind. The rest of the dinner continued quietly.

At dawn the following morning, Scipio bid farewell to his mother and his younger brother, Lucius. Scipio's mother wished the men a safe return to the city. General Varro's army gathered at the eastern gates of the city. Publius the Elder took his place at the front of his army and signaled the march to begin.

As Scipio and Laelius began their journey, leaving the city behind them, Laelius turned to Scipio: "For the Republic."

Scipio nodded gravely. "For the Republic."

Chapter Three

SWEAR THE SAME OATH—216 B.C.

Their destination was the town of Cannae. After two years of miserable defeats at the hands of the Carthaginians, Scipio and Laelius seemed to march in a funeral procession rather than a legion. Since leaving the city, the Roman war effort had suffered one tragedy after another. A Roman army pursuing Hannibal in Trebia was ambushed by Mago, one of his most trusted generals. Hannibal was able to continue southward into Tuscany, where General Flaminius took the risk of engaging with him in battle and paid for it. The Romans, including their valiant commander, were slaughtered along the banks of Lake Trasimene. Not only did fifteen thousand Roman troops and a prominent general perish, but the Carthaginians also ambushed Rome's relief force. Laelius and Scipio sometimes thought back to the bright winter they had spent in their beloved city, but many of their comrades said that since the slaughter at Lake Trasimene, mourning had overwhelmed Rome. It would have broken their hearts to return now.

After Hannibal defeated Flaminius's force at Trasimene, the city itself was in danger. Terrified, the citizens reelected Fabius Maximus as dictator instead of returning to their annual senate elections, which had been the original caveat of Fabius's rise to power. Fortunately, the people had also elected Lucius Paullus, Aemelia's father, and Gaius Varro, an experienced general, as consuls during the same election. Varro and Paullus agreed to lead an army against Hannibal, who was camped at Apulia. Varro's plan was to choke the Carthaginian general's army by surrounding it with a force of eighty thousand Roman and allied soldiers.

Laelius and Scipio had been in Pisa when they received a summons asking for the legion's most experienced infantrymen and cavalrymen. They received a second message not long after, directly from Paullus, specifically requesting that Scipio and Laelius be sent. They were two out of a thousand soldiers who joined Varro's forces east of Rome. Once they began speaking with other cavalrymen in Varro's army, they learned that the plans had changed.

"There's a garrison in this small town in the south called Cannae," an infantryman named Appius Claudius told them. "At least, there was."

"Hannibal?" Scipio guessed.

Claudius nodded. "Apparently he'd gotten wind of Varro's plan to surround the army and decided to force his hand. The garrison wasn't too large, but the commander is afraid that if we wait any longer, Hannibal will start taking out all the Roman outcroppings in the south. If he takes too many of those, Rome will lose every southern ally it has."

As the two friends marched toward Cannae, the men in their legion became increasingly excited and apprehensive about the impending battle. They would face the infamous Carthaginian general himself on the battlefield. He had a merciless reputation, and many of the men feared that if Rome did not win the day, they would never see their loved ones again. Scipio, however, was optimistic as ever. He had steadfast confidence in Rome's military prowess, even against the most ruthless general in recorded history.

Just before dawn, Laelius and Scipio caught a glimpse of the Carthaginian camp. The army moved into position on the other side of the Aufidus River. At first light, they could see the camp across the river stir to life. Scipio and Laelius took up their places on the right flank with the rest of the army's cavalry.

Paullus wandered by the pair. He leaned over to Scipio and said, "Let's pray that Fortuna smiles on us." He rested his hand on Scipio's shoulder before continuing on. It was abundantly clear how fond Paullus was of young Scipio.

Scipio looked to his friend. "For the Republic."

"For the Republic," Laelius agreed.

When the sun had risen fully, Scipio and Laelius were facing the seven thousand Spanish and Celtic cavalries. Both the horses and their riders were stout and wide, but muscled. Hasdrubal was at the head of Hannibal's cavalry. He stood tall and proud, the rays of the sun glinting against his armor and silhouetting his face. Higher up the hill, they could see an outline of Hannibal. Though he was too far away to make out clearly, his presence still made Scipio's blood boil.

The soldiers squared their footing. Their eyes shined with bloodlust. Some snarled toothy smirks at the Romans. The air was electric with anticipation. The hairs on Laelius's neck rose, and his mouth tasted metallic. The trumpet sounded, and the two armies crashed together.

The right flank immediately fell to shambles. The Spanish and Celtic cavalries outnumbered them nearly twofold. Laelius and Scipio quickly realized that they were surrounded by enemy horsemen. Stones and large hunks of lead rained down on them from the Carthaginian army. Laelius heard the crack of bone and Paullus shout in pain. Scipio turned and tried to find the general, but all they could see were enemy horses and shields. A Celtic warrior came barreling down toward Laelius, raising a heavy iron sword above his head. Laelius quickly slashed his side. A Spanish cavalryman tried spearing Laelius while his back was turned, but Scipio caught him in the stomach.

The Roman army slowly, painfully advanced up the incline, pushing Hannibal's army back. But the farther the Romans advanced, the more compressed their army became. Soon, Laelius and Scipio were shoulder-to-shoulder trying to dodge lances, blades, and spear points inches away. Neither one of them had enough room to angle their blades. Scipio inched around Laelius so that the two were back-to-back. They were able to maneuver themselves so that one could give the other enough space to pull back and stab forward while the other defended with his shield. Still, there was no sign of relief, or even a friendly face.

Suddenly, the Carthaginian infantrymen facing inward toward the center of Rome's army turned outward and began attacking the flanks. Hasdrubal and his cavalry began running the right flank into the river. The packed force of Roman soldiers burst into disparate companies engaging with whomever was attacking them. The army's entire formation fell into disarray within minutes. Meanwhile, Hasdrubal and his cavalry started to force the right flank into the river. The water began to run deep purple. The air filled with the nauseating scent of blood and upturned dirt. The compact mass of the melee pressed

Scipio and Laelius closer and closer to the water. If they did not act soon, they would be pushed into the water and perhaps trampled.

"It's hopeless!" Laelius shouted. "There are too many. We'll be slaughtered!"

Scipio looked at Laelius with a pained expression. He wanted to stay and fight to the end, but it was clear that Rome would not win the day. They would have to choose: die for their country now or fight another battle.

Scipio made the final call, slashing through the wall of Spanish and Celtic warriors until the two of them were at the water's edge. A Spanish rider immediately spotted them and charged through the water. Scipio picked up an enormous stone from the river and threw it. It caught the rider in the shoulder, causing him to drop his weapon. Laelius swung at him and sent him toppling from his horse. In just seconds, Laelius leapt onto the now-riderless steed and steered him back toward Scipio. Laelius helped his friend on the horse and the two turned to ride back into the heat of the battle.

But it was clear now that the battle had almost finished. Rome was no longer gaining any ground and the entire army had fractured. Hannibal's men were isolating small pockets of the army and cutting them down. His cavalrymen were pursuing those attempting to retreat and slaughtering them as they ran. Even the small Roman camp had been overrun.

"Hannibal is just going to destroy as much of the army as he can," Laelius murmured.

"Let's see if we can find anyone else who escaped," Scipio said.

Laelius directed them toward the hills. They abandoned the horse at the base and climbed into a grove of olive trees to hide.

Laelius sensed that something was not quite right and reached for his sword. Scipio placed his hand on the hilt of his sword as well. All of a sudden, the two of them saw movement in the grove a few feet away. They drew their weapons at the stranger.

"Scipio! Laelius!" Appius Claudius carefully made his way down the hill to them. "You survived!"

"We may be the only ones," Laelius said darkly.

"Not at all! There's a group of us further up the hill. We're going to make our way to a camp at Canusium to regroup."

Scipio and Laelius followed Claudius up the hill and discovered the stragglers who had managed to escape the violence. As night fell, more and more Roman soldiers joined the group until about four thousand of them were gathered on the hill among the trees.

"We should leave now, before the Carthaginians come looking for survivors," suggested Fabius the Younger, an older infantryman.

"Is there anyone else who might join us?" Claudius asked.

"The battle is over," a wounded soldier sighed. "If anyone else is left, they are lost or in Hannibal's hands."

"We'll have to be cautious," Fabius the Younger insisted. "The Carthaginians are out for blood. Even though they have won the battle, if they discover us, we're dead."

Claudius agreed, and took the lead. With Scipio and Laelius immediately behind, they began their careful journey over the hill toward Canusium.

As the four thousand men crept along the Tuscan hills, Laelius noticed a look of determination on Scipio's face. He seemed emboldened by his place at the head of this modest legion of stragglers. This region of Tuscany was littered with Hannibal's patrolmen. One misplaced step might expose them all. Any time that other men would freeze or shudder at the sounds of men or horses below, Scipio would touch his hand to his sword. He was ready should he need to defend these men. He would give his life for them if necessary. Laelius marveled at the transformation his friend had undertaken. He was the head of a pack of summer wolves who had survived the harsh winter.

Scipio was the first to catch sight of the camp at Canusium. The torchlight of the campsite burned low and earthy in the blue darkness of the night. The men quietly inched down the hill. Many were afraid that the Carthaginians had secretly followed them all this way—or worse, they had already taken the camp. There was only one way to find what awaited the men in Canusium.

Scipio and Laelius kept their hands at the ready as they approached the camp. A quick survey of the site yielded no Carthaginian ambush or soldiers lying in wait. The men gathered in the center of the camp.

"We aren't safe here," Fabius the Younger announced. "This camp is within easy reach of Hannibal's patrols. We will need to come up with a plan."

"We need a leader," someone suggested. There was a murmur of agreement throughout the crowd.

"I will lead us," Fabius the Younger announced.

"Why you?" Laelius shot back. "Claudius is the one who brought us all together, and he and Scipio have been at the head of the group for seven miles. They're the ones who kept us from being discovered." There was another murmur throughout the crowd.

Fabius the Younger shot a poisonous glare at Laelius. "I

have more military experience than either of them. I have been fighting the Carthaginians since the First War. I'm the only one with enough of a record."

Members of the crowd began to debate among themselves, which quickly escalated into shouts and threats.

Scipio projected above the crowd, "Why don't we put it to a vote?"

The crowd settled down. Scipio looked between his fellow soldiers.

"Our Republic was founded on the voice of the people being expressed through the election of their leaders," Scipio said. "Shouldn't we emulate that?"

Fabius the Younger appeared to protest, but conceded. Instead, he shot a look at Laelius so deadly that Laelius feared he might be turned to stone on the spot.

"Whom shall we nominate to lead us? I nominate Appius Claudius," one of the men shouted. Claudius glowed with flattery.

"I nominate myself," Fabius the Younger announced.

"I nominate Scipio," Laelius said.

"I will moderate the election," announced the soldier with the wounded shoulder. He made his way to the center of the crowd alongside the three candidates. "Given the size of those gathered at present, we will need two leaders. Those casting a vote for Fabius the Younger, say 'aye!'"

A loud "aye" echoed throughout the camp. Fabius the Younger stood with a satisfied smirk on his face.

"Those casting a vote for Appius Claudius, say 'aye!'"

An even louder "aye" boomed from the crowd.

The wounded soldier adjusted his shoulder and cleared his throat before continuing, "Those casting a vote for Publius Cornelius Scipio, say 'aye!'"

A hugely resounding "aye" shook the camp. Fabius the Younger was perhaps the most shaken.

The wounded soldier announced, "Our elected leaders are Appius Claudius and Publius Cornelius Scipio."

An immense cheer erupted from the crowd. Laelius looked to Scipio, whose pride made the torches behind him glow brighter.

The faction would stay the night at Canusium while Scipio and Claudius discussed their next move. A few men volunteered to go looking for survivors who might have been wandering about the Tuscan countryside. As the faction prepared their sleeping arrangements, the soldiers quickly split among their social classes. The nobles took up beds in the noblemen's chambers of the camp, while the artisans, farmers, and their apprentices found their own chambers.

Laelius loitered inside the commander's tent while Scipio and Claudius discussed their options. Around midnight, Claudius decided to take a walk around the camp and clear his head.

Scipio looked to Laelius with an apologetic expression. "You should get some rest."

Laelius shuffled indecisively. "It's all right. I would rather not leave you alone."

"I won't be alone. Claudius will be back quite soon."

Laelius must have betrayed a look of embarrassment, because Scipio asked, "What's the matter?"

"The farmers' quarters are far away from the commander's tent, and if anything should happen—if you should need me—"

"Laelius, you are my friend. You have the freedom to rest your head in whatever bed you choose as long as I am commander. But please get some sleep. You're no help to any of us exhausted."

Laelius nodded, wished his friend a goodnight, and made

his way to the noblemen's tents, which were much closer to the commander's tent.

As he walked past a large noblemen's tent, a voice determinedly whispering caught his ear. It sounded like Fabius the Younger. Something in his hushed tone implored Laelius to listen. He sneaked around to the side of the tent where the voice was loudest. He made sure that none of the lit torches would backlight his shadow to those within, and put his ear against the canopy.

"He's right, Metellus." Laelius recognized the voice as belonging to a nobleman named Caecilius. "Rome's defeat is imminent. You were there in the battlefield during the slaughter today. This army is a lost cause."

"How about what Scipio said about emulating Rome? What about our home?" asked someone whom Laelius figured was Metellus.

"Scipio is young and foolish," came Fabius the Younger's voice. "When Hannibal arrives at Rome's gates, he will burn the city to the ground. You won't have a home anymore. It's time we all accept that."

"We're good soldiers. We could volunteer ourselves as mercenaries to Iberian kings. We might still be fighting against Carthage and, besides that, we'll bring a huge salary home to our families. Our fathers built up noble houses. Everything they've given us—everything that is rightfully ours—is going to be taken away by some Carthaginian soldier as spoils of war," Caecilius insisted.

"Wouldn't your ancestors rather you grow the fortune they passed down to you than watch it all go up in flames in the pyre of defeat?" Fabius the Younger asked.

"We have a choice here," Caecilius said.

"You're right," Metellus said after a thoughtful pause. "So, what do we do?"

"I'll travel through the tents and inform any friendly ears to meet in your tent in an hour. Scipio and Claudius will have retired by then and we can plan our escape."

The tent rustled and Laelius dove into the shadows. He watched Fabius the Younger and Caecilius leave the tent and walk off. Once the sounds of their footsteps had faded, Laelius immediately ran back to the commander's tent and told Scipio everything he had overheard. When Scipio heard the noblemen's plan to desert, a white-hot rage entered his eyes. He took up his sword and bade Laelius and Claudius follow him. The three men marched past the noblemen's tents to the artisans' quarters and then the farmers' tents, waking all the men and instructing them to follow Scipio.

"Come with me, sword in hand, if you wish to save your country!" Scipio shouted. "The enemy's camp is nowhere more truly than in our own!"

His following had increased to more than twenty-five hundred men. Some nobles, awoken by the shouting, joined the mob behind Scipio. Their weapons, sinister-looking, glinted in the low torchlight. No one seemed to quite know what Scipio was up to, but they were all raring to defend their country behind their elected leader.

Scipio and his band burst into Metellus's tent. A large gathering of noblemen had already shown up. They stopped their discussion immediately and turned to the invading mob of soldiers with a look of utter shock. Laelius did not see Fabius the Younger in the tent with them.

Scipio raised his sword high above his head and announced in a booming voice: "I swear with all the passion of my heart that I shall never in all my life desert our mother country! I shall never permit any other citizen of Mother Rome to leave her in times of need, though the fight may be hard won. If I willingly break my oath to her, may Jupiter rain shame upon my head and upon my house, upon my family and all that I possess. Swear the same oath, Caecilius, and all others who are gathered here. Know that my sword is drawn against he who refuses."

The camp was silent. Laelius caressed the hilt of his sword. Should any of the noblemen gathered draw his sword against Scipio, Laelius was ready. But no one moved.

Caecilius looked across at Scipio. The torches reflected red in the commander's pitch-black pupils. Caecilius stood. He looked to his men and then back to Scipio. He bowed his head reverently and began reciting Scipio's oath.

The rest of the would-be deserters soon started to recite it along with him until every nobleman gathered was pledging their allegiance to Rome. Then, members of the crowd behind Scipio started to recite the same oath. Farmers and noblemen, Roman artisans and merchants, and allied mercenaries all joined in a single voice that echoed across the early morning Tuscan fields. As the last man spoke the final word, silence fell over the faction. Though the night's oil had almost burned away, the torches around Scipio seemed to shine brighter than ever.

One of the scouts who had gone searching for wandering soldiers returned just after dawn. He presented himself to the commanders.

"What news have you found," Claudius asked, "and where are the other scouts?"

"We came upon a group of Roman infantrymen who had also survived," the soldier said. "They were heading to Venusia to regroup with General Varro."

"General Varro survived as well?" Scipio brightened. "Was there any word on General Paullus?"

"He was with this group!" the soldier said excitedly. Scipio smiled with relief as the soldier continued. "He was wounded by a stone from a sling-thrower, but not badly. He should heal soon. The other scouts joined the group to continue on to Venusia, but I came back to tell the rest of the camp."

"Very well," Claudius said. "Thank you for your service."

The soldier bowed and departed.

Scipio turned to his co-commander. "We should ready the camp to march to Venusia. With General Varro and General Paullus still alive, perhaps this battle was not as immense a loss as we imagined."

"My thoughts exactly," Claudius agreed.

During the march to Venusia, Scipio was contemplative and spoke little. Laelius became worried for his friend. He could not imagine that the pressure of command had gotten to his head, so perhaps there was another matter on his mind. Once they arrived at the Roman camp, they were greeted with a huge celebration. But the army's reunion was bittersweet as the defeat at Cannae was still fresh in everyone's mind. Varro publicly thanked Scipio and Claudius for taking charge of the faction, applauding their natural leadership. Scipio accepted the thanks with gratitude, but remained quiet. Finally, Laelius approached him.

"What's on your mind?"

Scipio looked to his friend. "Hadn't you guessed?" Laelius shook his head. "There was one man who didn't take my oath."

Laelius's eyes widened. Of course! "Fabius the Younger."

Scipio nodded. "If what you heard was true, Fabius the

Younger orchestrated the desertion to undermine me and Claudius, but he was savvy enough not to show up at their meeting."

"Then we should expose him," Laelius insisted.

Scipio looked up into the sky thoughtfully. "Fabius Maximus is his father—the dictator of Rome now. Making a public enemy of Fabius the Younger would mean antagonizing the most powerful man in the Roman government." Scipio looked back into Laelius's eyes. "I'm leaving Varro's army to join my father in Spain. I can do more good there than here, but I can't risk leaving a snake like Fabius the Younger who might pounce at any moment."

"They will follow the oath you made them take, Scipio."

"Yes," Scipio sighed, "but venom is powerful. Fabius the Younger is dangerous, Laelius, and you and I are the only two people who know it."

"You want me to stay here," Laelius guessed. "You want me to stay in Varro's army to keep an eye on Fabius the Younger while you join your father."

Scipio nodded. The sad conclusion to the puzzle had come.

Laelius grabbed Scipio and pulled him into a tight hug. "Whatever your orders, I will follow," Laelius swore. This was his personal oath to Scipio.

Later that day, Laelius watched Scipio ride west into the sinking, liquefying sun.

Chapter Four

THE AGE OF SCIPIO—213 B.C.

Three years after Laelius had last seen Scipio, he found himself again at the door to his friend's home. Villa Scipio was just as Laelius had remembered it when he left its doors four years earlier. The statue of Vesta greeted him with open arms at the other end of the atrium as he entered the house. The unique and exotic aromas that filled its halls had grown stronger in late spring. The gorgeous tile floors were newly polished and sparkling. The murals on the walls had been touched up and repainted. If it weren't for the carefully curated garden, a stranger might believe that the house had been built just weeks ago.

Scipio was sitting with his father in the tablinum. He caught sight of Laelius and ran to him, folding his friend into a huge bear hug. Scipio stepped back and regarded Laelius happily. The two men had been fighting for the past years with legions that seemed to pass one another like ships in the night without ever intersecting. Laelius was finally able to look on his friend's face once again.

"It is so good to see you, my friend!" Scipio said.

"It is good to see you, too."

"You look well. You grew out your beard."

"Yes," Laelius laughed, scratching his chin. "You still shave?"

"Yes. I used to be the only one in the legion, but I told them that I'd grabbed enough Celtic riders by the chin to know you should give your enemies a smooth surface. It caught on."

The two friends strolled toward the garden. A fat, pollen-laden bee buzzed past Laelius's ear.

"Were you discussing the election with your father?" Laelius asked.

Scipio nodded. "It seems like all I talk about these days is the aedileship." Off of Laelius's funny look, he added, "What is it?"

"You're getting married in two days."

Scipio chuckled, smiling to himself as if he had almost forgotten. "I wish my mind were preoccupied with the wedding, but the aedileship is all anyone cares to mention. If it were up to me, my day with Aemelia wouldn't be marred by such political conversations."

They sat down on a marble bench, upsetting a butterfly that had been sunbathing.

"An aedileship isn't such a prestigious position," Scipio reflected, "but it is the sort of position that leads to more prestigious consulships and high-level military commands. Because I am the firstborn of a prominent Roman household, it is time I consider my political career." Scipio sighed. "I only wish the timing were better."

"But you're running because you want to?" Laelius asked. "Not for your father?"

Scipio looked at Laelius, perplexed. "I am running for the Republic. I am running because my father is right when he says that the values of the Roman Republic must not be forgotten in a time of war, when men like him cannot afford to be in the senate chambers."

Laelius took in his friend's words. A warm spring breeze blew across his cheek, and with it came the faint sound of the busy city streets. The people of Rome could use men like Scipio to lead them.

He nudged Scipio. "What about Aemelia?"

Scipio laughed. "She has been my only relief from all this political discourse."

"Well, then let's make sure your vows don't turn into campaign promises on the day," Laelius said, standing.

He helped Scipio to his feet and the two resumed their stroll.

The Baths of Pax was the most luxurious bathhouse in the city. Esteemed men gathered here to relax, exercise, groom, dine, mingle, attend lectures by renowned thinkers and intellectuals, and conduct business. It was known as the Baths of Pax because it was a place in which enemies could leave their differences outside its walls and speak to one another as friends. This bathhouse became particularly popular as Rome's annual elections approached. Candidates could escape the political ire that followed them during daily life and become anonymous patrons alongside their fellow countrymen.

Laelius and Scipio pressed their backs against the cool marble wall inside the tepidarium room. The large crystal pool stretched out in front of them. A relief of Neptune emerging from the waves in a horse-drawn chariot gazed at them from the opposite end. They had just visited the caldarium, the hottest of Pax's many baths, and sweat still dripped from their curls. The cold marble against their backs felt refreshing and reinvigorated their entire bodies.

Laelius glanced over at his friend. Scipio certainly looked older than the young leader riding west from Venusia. His face had hardened into a man's with a chiseled jaw, proud Roman nose, and curious brow. His mouth had retained its youthful rise at the corners, giving him a resting expression of amusement. His eyes, however, were older than all the rest of him. His dark pupils showed immense depth and his irises were faded brown like worn leather. However, it was evident that Scipio would retain his youthful looks long into his adulthood.

Scipio's father entered the tepidarium with a band of other men. This consisted of Scipio's uncle Gnaeus, General Paullus, and Scipio's brother Lucius. The group made their way to the two men. Paullus bade an attendant fetch them goblets of wine.

"Tomorrow's the day," Publius the Elder said, sitting beside his son. "You'll be a married man this time tomorrow."

The wine arrived and Paullus proposed a toast. "May your marriage be long and prosperous, and may the joining of our families be blessed under Venus and Jupiter. We are on the verge of witnessing the merging of two great houses." The men all drank. Almost immediately, Paullus spoke again. "Do you feel prepared for the election, Scipio?"

Scipio shifted on the wooden bench and nodded, but his future father-in-law was unconvinced.

"You are technically three years too young to run for an aedileship," said Paullus. "Have you considered waiting until you become legal age?"

"Cornelius Scipio is a better fit for an aedileship than men twice his age," Gnaeus interrupted. "He has performed more brave acts on behalf of the Republic than most consuls."

"I agree, but this isn't about his actions. It's about the simple and undeniable fact of his age," Paullus said.

"I'd like to see someone dispute his candidacy for such a minor technicality," Gnaeus scoffed.

"How can you deny the possibility?"

"Paullus," Scipio's father interrupted, "today is a day of celebration. Let's not become bogged down in current events and political speech."

Scipio looked to his father gratefully. Publius the Elder smiled proudly back.

"Scipio has shown more experience, bravery, intelligence, and intuition than many men I know," he said. "The Roman people will see that and cast their votes accordingly."

"You have an impressive trust in the habits of the Roman people," Paullus retorted, then softened, adding, "I hope that Scipio leads with the same conviction."

Publius the Elder raised his goblet and toasted, "May Fortuna bless our many endeavors as one family. May she bless the two lovers who bring us together. *Feliciter!*"

"*Feliciter!*" they echoed, and drank to Scipio and Aemelia. The wine continued to flow throughout the rest of the evening.

Villa Paullus, where the first part of the wedding was held, was similar to Villa Scipio in the glamorous décor, though more traditional. Their atrium was filled with olive and fig trees. Fragrant hyacinths and violets dotted the paths to the other rooms in the household. Newly planted white roses framed the altar that was placed in the center of the sunny atrium and covered in a pristine white cloth. Scipio stood between Laelius and his father to the right of the altar. The rest of those gathered in the atrium bisected the villa into two halves: the Scipios and the Paulluses. An even larger crowd of friends and well-wishers awaited them outside of the house. Tears already filled Scipio's mother's eyes.

Aemelia appeared out of the room that she had stayed in since childhood. She wore a white tunic held to her shoulders by floral pendants. Her long dark hair was parted into six strands and braided at the top of her head in a beautiful, intricate design. According to tradition, the women in the household had painstakingly crafted the braided design using a victorious gladiator's iron spearhead. She was crowned with a wreath of marjoram and wore a translucent red veil. Laelius might not have recognized her save for the confident smirk behind the red veil. She cradled a collection of small girl's toys in her arms. She placed these toys onto the altar and knelt, putting her hands on the altar.

"I offer these to Vesta, goddess of the hearth, and Janus, god of the threshold. These were my most beloved things as a child. As I loved these as a girl, so shall I love my husband as a woman. As I step beyond my old threshold and take up a new hearth, I pray their blessing follow me into my new home," she said, and then stood.

Aemelia's mother and the other women of the household offered bowls of fruit, vegetables, and grain to the household gods, also wishing for their blessing on Aemelia's departure to a new house. Her father took her hand and Scipio stood beside her at the altar. General Paullus placed his daughter's hands into Scipio's. Scipio squeezed them tightly, making Aemelia smile.

"I am now your family. We are one," said General Paullus.

A huge roar of "*Feliciter!*" and "*Talassio!*" erupted from those gathered. The altar was quickly cleared away and replaced with tables for a luxurious wedding feast: platters of immense silver eels and black lampreys, fragrant lamb chops, seasoned fish, bright jewel-like fruits, crisp vegetables, and golden bread still steaming from the oven. The tables were decorated with garlic knots and sage, symbols of protection and the health of the heart. Endless jugs of rich, ruby wine filled the glasses of all those in attendance. Laelius noted that the guests gathered to celebrate Scipio and Aemelia's marriage were some of Rome's most noteworthy figures. Members of all of Rome's noble families, senate consuls, political personalities, respected intellectuals, and generals from the military were present at the banquet.

The newlyweds had not seemed to release one another's hands since they were joined. They were seated side by side in two large wooden chairs, spending most of the meal whispering and giggling to one another. Guests sporadically toasted "*Feliciter!*" to Scipio and Aemelia, prompting a wave of toasts throughout the crowd. Many of the noblemen in attendance approached the newlyweds and briefly wished them a fruitful and prosperous marriage.

One nobleman, an older patriarch from the Fabian family, stood before Scipio and inquired, loudly enough for those nearby to clearly understand, "Cornelius Scipio, I congratulate you on your marriage to such a lovely creature and welcome you into the world of men, but I caution you not to get ahead of yourself."

Scipio smiled. "Thank you, sir—"

"After all, don't you find it a bit reckless to run for the aedileship at such a young age?" the nobleman interrupted. "No one your age has ever been elected to such a title. The common law even discourages it."

"I don't think my political career should encroach on a

day dedicated to the union of two homes," Scipio responded, and turned to Aemelia, hoping this would end the nobleman's probing.

"Aemelia-now-Scipio," the nobleman said, now addressing Scipio's wife, "wouldn't you say your husband's actions are reckless?"

"No, I would not," Aemelia informed the nobleman without missing a beat. "In fact, I believe that no one could do the job better than he could."

The nobleman muttered and returned to his seat, unable to find fodder sufficient to feed the flame he wished to cultivate. Laelius was delighted by Aemelia's curtness. Never before had he seen a wife so dedicated to her husband, and she was less than one day into the job. Everyone else who had overheard the exchange was visibly impressed as well. Even Scipio beamed, leaning over to whisper thanks to her.

"I told you," she said matter-of-factly, "we are one."

Once the feast had ended with a delicious dessert of sweet breads and sticky figs, some of the guests grabbed torches and led the bride, the groom, and their guests out of Villa Paullus. The wedding procession marched through the sapphire-dusk city streets. Crowds gathered shouting "*Talassio*!" or singing raunchy, obscene songs and poetry. Laelius led the procession, carrying the wedding torch burning brightest. Finally, they arrived at the door of Villa Scipio. Having reached their destination, Laelius threw the torch into the crowd. Gnaeus caught it and cheered, having been blessed with the promise of long life. Aemelia dipped a white cloth into a bowl of oil and fat and rubbed it into the doorposts. Then Scipio gently lifted her and carried her over the threshold into her new home, eliciting cheers from the crowd. Now, the real celebration would begin!

The attendants to Villa Scipio came forth with wine and bowls overflowing with more fruit. A miniature marriage bed intended for the bride and groom's spirits had been built in the garden, decorated with more roses and hyacinths. Music played. The newlyweds performed a traditional dance in which the bride flew into her mother's arms and her new husband tore her away into his. The guests laughed and sang and cheered for not only the newlyweds, but their own fortune as well. As good luck rained upon the newlyweds to overflowing, the guests felt that they, too, would have a more prosperous future after basking in the celebration.

Near the end of the night, Laelius, who had ingested a great deal of wine throughout the day, was congratulating Scipio yet again when Scipio's father and uncle approached them.

"We've just received word from some of our Spanish allies," his father explained. "Insurrections have popped up throughout some of the tribes loyal to Rome. Gnaeus and I must return to stabilize the region before they turn over to Carthage. I am sorry to say that I will not be able to be in the city for the aedileship election." He placed his hand on Scipio's shoulder. "Good luck, my boy."

Scipio nodded solemnly as his father and uncle exited quietly through the crowd. He was visibly shaken by his father's sudden departure. Such deep despondence entered Scipio's features that Laelius wondered if his friend really wanted to be an aedile at all. Perhaps his father's pride and belief in Scipio had brought the ambitious young man thus far, and without his father's presence, Scipio saw the true difficulty of the endeavor. Aemelia, who had overheard the interaction and detected her husband's uncertainty, slipped her hand into her husband's and stroked his cheek. She kissed him gently on the lips.

The final ceremony, the ritual of water and fire, concluded the evening. A large brass bowl of water and a small brazier of newly ignited fire were placed side by side in front of the effigy of Vesta. Scipio stood beside his beloved as she knelt down and touched both the water and fire, symbolizing her role as keeper of the hearth. The two then wished their guests good night, and made off to their marriage bed followed by the cheers of friends, family, and loved ones.

"This is absolutely ridiculous," one of the senators shouted. "The common law is quite clear: The age at which one is eligible to run for an aedileship is twenty-five years. Publius Cornelius Scipio is twenty-two. He is not eligible, and therefore cannot be considered."

Laelius watched his friend stand steadfast against the harsh words and even harsher gazes bearing down on him from the consuls overseeing the annual aedileship elections. They had gathered in the forum to submit Scipio as a candidate to the People's Tribunes, electorate parties of the senate. Fabius Maximus sat in the center of the Tribunes and listened. To think only weeks ago Scipio had been happily spending his honeymoon picking wildflowers with Aemelia. Now, he faced these men with the stance of a soldier, but a look in his eyes like a child who had been unjustly accused of theft.

The consuls had always scared Laelius. To him, they seemed like more than men. Many of them were ancient, with a small ring of ash, once hair, sprinkled around the crown of their heads and great, grumpy mouths containing too-large teeth. It seemed the flesh of their faces and capacity for positive expression had shrunk with age. They carried themselves like ogres, lumbering about their kingdom with the threat of a club that would politically crush you if you crossed them. It was as if the job itself had turned these men to monsters. The consuls were not all this way, of course. Many of them were young patriarchs of great families, as Scipio would likely be one day if he played his cards right.

Lucius Paullus stood beside Scipio and put his hand on his son-in-law's shoulder. He addressed the senator who had just spoken. "Scipio is more than qualified to be an aedile. His presence in our government would be more than a privilege; it's a necessity. We are at war—"

"Thank you for informing us," another consul interrupted.

Paullus's tone only became more accusatory. "Publius and Gnaeus Scipio are indispensable generals who have been fighting tirelessly to keep Hannibal from our doorstep. We have all benefitted from their protection. They have made the decision to sacrifice the two patriarchs of the Scipio family—which, may I remind you, was a family instrumental in the founding of our Republic—in order to protect this Republic. Should they both perish on the battlefield, Publius Cornelius Scipio, no matter his age, will become the patriarch of one of Rome's greatest families. Because Publius and Gnaeus have been fighting for Rome, the Scipios' voice has been missing from the government, and that is unacceptable."

"If I may, Paullus," Scipio said, placing his hand on his father-in-law's shoulder, "I know that my father and uncle are not looking for praise or even recognition for their military campaigns in Spain. They are fighting because it is their duty to fight for the Republic. With all due respect, consuls, I believe that the people of the Republic, the people that my father and uncle are fighting to protect, should be allowed to decide on their leadership."

The tribunes began to whisper among themselves. Laelius tried to catch Scipio's eye with a hopeful look.

One of the senators to Fabius Maximus's left announced, "Our tribune opposes Publius Cornelius Scipio's eligibility for aedileship."

"As does ours," a senator to Fabius Maximus's right agreed.

"But consuls—" Scipio tried.

"Fabius, dismiss this impudent child," the first senator insisted.

"I would like Scipio to stand for election."

The voice came from the back of the forum. Laelius, along with the rest of those gathered, turned to find Metellus with a defiant expression on his face.

"As would I," said another nobleman standing with Metellus.

"This not your place to decide," the senator insisted.

By now, however, a crowd had begun to gather in the forum. More noblemen began insisting that Scipio be allowed to run for the aedileship. Metellus and others ushered even more men into the crowd, telling them of Scipio's incredible leadership and military record. Many recognized his name from years back when he had rescued his father from certain death. The crowd chanted their support for Scipio to run.

Feeling the crowd's fervor, Fabius Maximus held up his hand, and the voices quieted. "Publius Cornelius Scipio, despite his youth, will be permitted to run for an aedileship."

He instructed the first senator who had opposed Scipio to run the election. Humiliated, the senator announced, "Those in favor of electing Publius Cornelius Scipio to aedile, say "aye.""

The "aye" was deafening.

~

Much of politics is made up of relationships and the preservation of the status quo. As such, Scipio's tumultuous and unconventional election to aedile did not win him many friends in the Roman government. From the first day, Scipio realized that he had enemies in the government conspiring against him. He would often come upon whispering enclaves of consuls who immediately stopped their discussion in his presence. Even if they were civil to Scipio politically, he found himself being immediately criticized. His adoration of Hellenic culture since his early days surfaced among the consuls and it became a sensation throughout the senate. He was criticized for wearing his robes in the Greek fashion and filling his home with Hellenic artwork and statuary. Even his political ideology was dismissed as "impossibly Greek," despite the fact that the only position Scipio was quite sure of was his loyalty to the Roman Republic.

There was also the matter of his wife. Aemelia, who had always been an independent girl, took to married life with an equally defiant gusto. She quickly became a well-known figure in Roman society, hosting extravagant salons with other wives and important Roman women, as well as riding around the city. No wife was as free as Aemelia Scipio, many people remarked, and not all with a complimentary tone. Many of the consuls thought it poor conduct for the wife of an aedile to come and go as she pleased. More traditional Romans insisted that the wife's place was in the home. She was even accused of acting like an empress, showing off her family's wealth with expensive jewels and tunics and riding through the city in a "gaudy" carriage. Her response to this accusation was that Roman women were more often seen as sacrificial objects than people capable of enjoying life's finery. She was not an empress, but a new type of Roman woman. Though many Roman women felt empowered by Aemelia, her response was not taken well by her critics who held up traditional roles in the household.

No one was a bigger fan of Aemelia than Scipio, and she was his most adamant supporter. Aemelia was a much-needed respite from the unceasing backlash Scipio felt in the government. Together, the two built a happy home filled with beauty and laughter. It was only with Aemelia that Scipio could forget about the war threatening Rome every day. Laelius would often join the happy couple for meals in Villa Scipio. Though Aemelia was criticized in the public sphere for neglecting her home, her presence had a significant impact on Villa Scipio. The home had a brighter, more youthful energy. Even the old Hellenic sculptures that Scipio had moved into the home seemed rejuvenated. Aemelia hired a painter to accent many of the home's murals with gold paint, which imbued the whole house with more warmth and splendor.

As Laelius reclined for another meal with his friends, however, he could see that Aemelia's touch did not extend far beyond the home's walls.

Scipio dragged his bread through the olive oil. "New Carthage is Hannibal's stronghold in Spain. If we take it, Carthage loses its hold on the Spanish tribes. If we don't, Hannibal's generals will continue to attack Roman allies, kill our troops, and turn the tribes against us. We could oust Carthage off European soil, but still the consuls refuse to listen to reason."

"Did your father send another letter?" Laelius asked.

Aemelia shot him a warning look, confirming his suspicion.

Scipio sighed. "It seems like every day brings bad news: more Spanish tribes that have switched over to the Carthaginians or more Roman troops killed or lost or captured. Each step that my father and uncle take south of the Ebro River is filled with more terror than the last. Still, they're making progress in Spain! They are getting closer and closer to New Carthage! Yet, all the senate focuses on is Hannibal."

"But Hannibal is in Italy," Aemelia ventured.

"If Hannibal wanted to take the city, he would have. Our defenses would put up a good fight, but not good enough that it would deter him from a siege," Scipio said.

"Then why doesn't he attack the city?" Aemelia asked.

"I don't know," Scipio mumbled. It was clear that Scipio had been meditating on this question for quite some time. "All I can think is that Hannibal must have a different plan in mind. For instance, he may be trying to take down our allies in neighboring regions—like Spain—first, to eliminate the chance of Rome regrouping."

"And the senate isn't interested in concentrating more of their forces in Spain?" Laelius inquired.

"'Stay put' is what the consuls say," Scipio growled. "It's Fabius Maximus's strategy: all defense and procrastination."

After dinner, Laelius met with Scipio in the garden. The two men sat on stone benches opposite one another. Scipio looked down at his feet.

"You don't seem to be enjoying your tenure as aedile," Laelius noted.

"Do you remember when you asked why I was running for the aedileship? Whether it was my father's influence or my own?"

"Yes. You said you felt it was your duty to the Roman people."

"Yes," Scipio said, "exactly! The Roman people elected me, but I feel as if I'm doing them no good. I'm not getting anything done as an aedile, and it's torture watching the senior senators sit on their hands and twiddle their thumbs while Roman citizens are fighting and dying for their country."

"Maybe you just need to give it some time," Laelius suggested. "The city wasn't built in a day."

The more time that Scipio spent as an aedile, the more frustrated he became with the government. The consuls were all petty and selfish. His fellow aediles, the lowest position within the government, only cared about climbing the rungs of the senate. The older senators were conniving and mostly discussed subverting their political enemies in hushed huddles in the halls outside the senate chambers. They swapped favors to help their sons climb to more prominent positions. They engaged in long debates and created laws just to undermine one another. Meanwhile, food was being heavily rationed in the city as Hannibal leeched local farms across Italy. Imports from Spain had stopped completely.

If there was one thing that the consuls agreed on, it was that war was hell and they would do anything to avoid it. As long as a man served his country through the government, he would not have to serve in the military, so consuls would hold special elections, come up with convoluted loopholes in the laws, and oust other men from their positions in order to ensure their sons, grandsons, and nephews places in the government. Meanwhile, nearly every day Scipio received letters from his father detailing the fight in Spain.

One year after Scipio's election to the aedileship, Laelius received a message summoning him to Villa Scipio. After dinner with Scipio and his family, and once Aemelia had gone off, the two men were left alone to talk.

Scipio solemnly turned to Laelius. "I have decided to go back into the field," he said. "My father told me of a position commanding a legion at Capua. There, I will be able to help him and my uncle in their military efforts. I cannot stand feeling this stagnant." He leaned back in his chair, furrowing his brow. "I will be helping the people of Rome much more out there as commander of the cavalry than I ever could in the senate chambers. I could make real advances toward winning this war." Scipio looked squarely into his friend's eyes. "I want you to come with me, Laelius—if you'd like to."

Laelius smiled at his friend in the darkness. "Of course. It's boring to live in the lap of luxury."

Scipio laughed. "For the Republic."

"For the Republic," Laelius agreed.

When the two had laid out the plans for their departure and finished off their wine, Laelius bid Scipio farewell. He came upon Aemelia in the garden, staring up to Vesta's placid face. She looked lovely and sad in the moonlight.

"Did he tell you?" Laelius asked.

"He told me two days ago that he planned on returning to the war," Aemelia told him. Though her composure was stately, it was clear she was upset.

Laelius felt for her. Scipio loved her deeply, but even she knew that he was not yet ready to remain in the city. While the other senators did all they could to avoid the reality of the war, Scipio fled into it.

"Don't worry, Aemelia," Laelius told her. "I won't let anything happen to him."

As he walked home through the empty city streets, Laelius could not help but feel excited. The two friends would be back on the field together again for the first time in six years. Hannibal's men didn't stand a chance.

Laelius and Scipio left the next morning for Capua.

A few months later, Scipio and Laelius met in the commander's tent at Puteoli to prepare for the legion's next move. They had chased Hannibal's forces across Naples. The small skirmishes with the Carthaginian general's army had been modestly successful for the legion, giving Scipio the confidence to make a more significant strike at Hannibal. Scipio had relocated from Capua to the seaside town to give the legion a more strategic location that was both less exposed to Hannibal's landlocked forces and easier for acquiring provisions from Rome via ships. Now, with the salty sea breeze tickling the canvas of the tent, Scipio and Laelius discussed moving the legion further inland to take the offensive against their enemy.

The provisions that Scipio's legion received included not only food, fodder for horses, new weapons, and materials for blacksmiths and seamstresses, but also people. These provisions arrived much faster and had a lower likelihood of being captured by enemy forces traveling by sea than land. The military messenger who arrived with an official letter for Scipio, for instance, arrived a whole day earlier by traveling on ship than he might have on foot or horseback. When he arrived at the commander's tent, he removed his helmet and greeted the commander as any soldier would his superior.

"A message for you, sir," the messenger said.

"Yes?" Scipio inquired.

Suddenly, the messenger could not speak. He had never met the man who had, at just a year older than the messenger was now, sliced through a mob of Carthaginian spearmen and saved his father. The boy was struck by Scipio's humanity. He did not look like a god or the progeny of one, but simply a great man in a commander's uniform. Yet there was something more, something about Scipio's carriage that struck the messenger with a great deal of awe. Laelius saw it in the messenger's changed expression.

"Well?" Scipio asked.

The young messenger coughed awkwardly and scratched under his armpit where the horsehair on his helmet had been irritating him. "Unfortunate news, Commander," the messenger began. "Publius the Elder and Gnaeus Scipio have perished at Castulo."

Something broke. It was as if Scipio had been a great mirror that had, without warning, cracked down the center.

"What?"

"They were betrayed by a group of Spanish allies. The Carthaginians murdered both generals, led by a General Massinissa. All the Roman troops in Spain have now fled north of the Ebro River."

Scipio sat down, utterly shocked. He dismissed the messenger, who left as awkwardly as he had come.

"Scipio?" Laelius said gently, but hot tears had already begun to leak from the corners of his friend's eyes.

Scipio's face became flush, and then red like a sunburn. He began to scream, cursing Jupiter, Mars, and any other god he could think of. He broke down into hysterical sobs and shouts. Laelius tried to comfort his friend, but nothing could be done. Scipio dove deep into despair almost instantaneously.

Laelius had always known his friend to be passionate, but also levelheaded and reflective. He had never seen Scipio so inconsolable, and he never would again.

Laelius stood watch over his friend all night. Scipio did not stop screaming and sobbing until the moon was high in the air and the tragedy had overwhelmed him into sleep. Laelius lifted him into a comfortable position. The sea breeze played through Scipio's curls. Laelius looked out the open mouth of the tent and up at the stars in search of two new constellations.

Chapter Five

THE YOUNG COMMANDER—210 B.C.

The duty of a house is to stand steadfast as its residents come, change, and eventually depart. Villa Scipio had remained standing through generations of Scipios. It had allowed midwives, tutors, Rome's greatest generals, wedding parties, and funeral processions in and out of its doors. It had witnessed life play out its bittersweet song with variations on its familiar theme again and again. It was the role of life to transfigure, progress, and fade while the house filled its walls, doorways, floors, and corners with memories. Villa Scipio, like its inhabitants, took its vocation very seriously and performed exceedingly well.

For months after they had returned to Rome, Laelius would find Scipio staring at odd corners of the house or across the atrium into the tablinum, where his father had spent most of his time. He would pick up insignificant objects—dinner plates, spoons, pillows, paper—as if they held the answers to the universe. His father's war maps were all placed in a sealed, waterproof wooden chest, and Scipio would only remove them one at a time, meticulously placing the previous one back in the chest before removing the next one he wanted to consult.

Life sometimes takes on a cyclical dance. Aemelia gave birth to their first child a month after Laelius and Scipio arrived. It was without question that they would name him after his grandfather and, just as Aemelia's presence in Villa Scipio had filled the house with new light, the birth of Publius made its aura more youthful. The house adjusted itself from the home of a newlywed couple to the home of a child. As his son grew old enough to move on his own, Scipio would proudly watch him crawl and explore every nook and cranny. He found immense joy in witnessing his son discover a bug in the garden or encounter a songbird for the first time. His eyes were reopened to the novelty and beauty of the world that children see so easily.

The birth of his son was far from the only thing on Scipio's mind. After the funeral services honoring his father and uncle, the senate sent Gaius Claudius Nero, one of Rome's most experienced military officers, with a small force of his own to join what was left of Publius the Elder's legion in Spain. When Publius the Elder and his brother were betrayed, seven years of progress, everything that they worked toward, had been wiped away in a single afternoon. Nero's only course of action was to stabilize the troops north of the Ebro. As the months marched on, Nero gave no suggestion of an attempt to venture south and regain the territory that was lost during the Battle of Castulo. Scipio had been fighting tirelessly to convince the senate to agree to a plan that would send his father's former legion south toward the Carthaginian stronghold of New Carthage. But as New Carthage got stronger every day, most consuls saw Spain as a lost cause.

Each day, Laelius walked with Scipio to the forum or the senate chambers. Sometimes they visited bathhouses where they knew senators would be in order to appeal to them. "I feel like I'm walking in his footsteps," Scipio told Laelius one day. "He was always advocating for Spain. He knew that the Iberian Peninsula was important to Carthage, and when they established New Carthage, he only fought harder for Rome's Spanish allies. Now I'm carrying on where he left off."

Walking in his father's footsteps emboldened Scipio more and more. Laelius noticed that whenever Scipio came back from the senate having been unable to convince the consuls, he was only more determined. Laelius was never quite sure whether it was the memory objects reminding him of his father, the innocent vivacity of his newborn son, or something innate to Scipio himself, but during that grueling, frustrating year in the city, Scipio never once lost his spirit.

If there was one thing that Scipio believed in above all else, it was Fortuna. Fortuna had kept him alive thus far, had given him a devoted wife and loving friend, had overseen the healthy birth of his son, and, a year after he left Naples to appeal to the Roman Senate, had created a proconsulship to lead the Roman legions in Spain. Fortuna had also given the proconsulship such a fearful stigma that no other man wanted to run for the position. As most of the noblemen had dismissed Spain as a lost cause alongside the senators, any position that sent a man to Spain was considered a death sentence. If Publius the Elder, one of the preeminent military leaders of the First War, perished attempting to conquer the region, following in his footsteps had to be suicidal.

Though no one else wanted to take the position, it would not be easy for Scipio to be elected, either. Given his months of campaigning and appeals, it was no secret to the consuls that Scipio would venture south of the Ebro if he were given command of Rome's Spanish legions. Many consuls believed this to be a reckless course of action, and Scipio's enemies in the senate fought adamantly to keep him out. Scipio was all but formally excluded from running for the position. If his tumultuous tenure as aedile had taught Scipio anything, it was that a controversial election would hurt his political future. With his father and uncle gone, Scipio could not risk ostracizing his family politically, so he decided to tread lightly around the proconsulship. Fortuna was frustratingly fickle.

Scipio finally convinced Fabius Maximus to confer with him separately about the position, and asked Laelius to join them. They met in a small room off the large senate chambers. Two consuls accompanied Fabius Maximus, with a third on the way. Scipio decided to begin without waiting for the third man to appear.

"You have heard my appeals to the other consuls for the past year. You know my dedication to the preservation of Rome's hold on Iberian Peninsula. There is no better fit for this proconsulship than me," Scipio said.

"Let me make something very clear." For a man famous for his procrastination, Fabius Maximus had no issue getting right to the point. "We are opening up this proconsulship because Nero is one of the Republic's most important military leaders and Rome needs him in the fight against Hannibal, not wasting his time in Spain. The proconsul is not meant to make any advance in Spain."

"But that is what I have been saying—advancement in Spain is not a waste of time. Rome's hold on the region—"

"—is gone!" Fabius Maximus insisted. "We lost the south of Spain to Carthage when we lost your uncle and father."

"Which is why it is so crucial to target that region," Scipio insisted.

Someone entered behind him. Fabius Maximus's eyes lit up.

"Ah, you're here. Please, sit beside me." Fabius Maximus gestured to the seat at his right.

Scipio and Laelius watched Fabius the Younger take his place at his father's right hand.

"I didn't realize you had become a consul," Scipio growled at his would-be saboteur.

"Father required me," Fabius the Younger smirked.

Scipio's mouth hardened.

Laelius jumped in. "Nobody else wants the position. Every other Roman half as capable as Scipio thinks it's a death wish."

"Perhaps you should heed their prudence," Fabius the Younger said.

"You need me to run," Scipio implored.

"You must fancy yourself exceedingly important, Scipio, if you believe that the Republic *needs* you. Your father had more years of experience, greater military victories, and a better understanding of leadership than you do, and Rome carries on without him," Fabius the Younger spat, jabbing eloquent knives into Scipio's armor.

"You can't keep me from running," Scipio snarled.

"No, but a proconsulship stresses, above all else, loyalty to the Republic, and any unapproved action he were to take in the line of duty would reflect gravely on the proconsul, his house, his legacy, and his ancestors," Fabius Maximus said.

"What are you saying?" Scipio whispered.

"Even if you're elected," Fabius the Younger chirped, "you won't take the legion south of the Ebro or anywhere near New Carthage. The senate will never approve it."

With that, Fabius Maximus and his cohorts excused themselves. Laelius and Scipio had no choice but to head home.

Back at Villa Scipio, Aemelia was far along in her second pregnancy. Though she had felt lonely and depressed and had been prone to frequent bouts of sickness during her pregnancy with Publius, she approached these nine months like a soldier. She knew the beast now, and was determined to conquer it with no cost to her own happiness. Scipio's presence in the house during this pregnancy also helped, improving both her mood and providing two more hands—four, when Laelius was around—at her disposal.

Since Scipio and Laelius had gone off to fight in Capua, Aemelia had only become more famous in Roman society. She was renowned for her lush, extravagant salons attended by Roman noblewomen. She had found a great deal of solidarity, joy, and love in these other women, and it was they who had helped her the most during her first pregnancy. Even with Scipio at home, Aemelia continued hosting these salons. The other noblewomen excitedly awaited another invitation to Villa Scipio, and not only because of the sumptuous food that Aemelia would bring to the women or the chance to spend more time in the house's famous garden. Aemelia Scipio's salons were the only venue in which the noblewomen of Rome could speak frankly about politics, current events, and the trials and tribulations of their homes and families. Every woman who entered that space found strength within the other women gathered, and Aemelia's bold yet caring nature left them feeling proud and happy to be Roman women as they made their way back to their own hearths.

Scipio often avoided these salons, not out of some childish fear of the feminine, but out of respect for the space that Aemelia and the other women had created for their own empowerment. However, while those gathered in Aemelia's salons were women, they were also Romans. Many of the women were wives, mothers, daughters, aunts, and nieces of consuls or military men and were personally interested in the progression of the war.

After his meeting with Fabius Maximus, Scipio had been quiet. He hadn't said a word about the meeting when he and Laelius climbed the steps of Villa Scipio. As they entered the atrium, a crowd of curious faces greeted the two men.

"*Mi amore*," Aemelia projected from the far end of the crowd of noblewomen, "I didn't realize you would be home so soon!" She was seated on a couch overflowing with cushions to support any strain on her back. Two of the women helped her to her feet and guided her over to her husband. Her belly protruded so far beyond the small woman's shoulders that she could barely hug her beloved, and instead offered a passionate kiss. "We were just discussing some current events."

"Good news is so hard to come by," said a woman Laelius recognized as Aemelia's sister-in-law, Papiria. "There's so much paranoia around Hannibal and his army. It's difficult to know whether what I hear is really the truth. What do you think, Scipio? Is Hannibal really as close as they say?"

Scipio shifted uncomfortably. "I have been in the city for a year. I'm sure many of your husbands are in the field and can provide you with more up-to-date information."

"But our husbands won't tell us anything," another woman in a peach tunic piped up. "They don't want to worry us with talk of war, but the fact is, we are worried. Every day you hear more and more about how gruesome this war has become. Please, Scipio, give us some hope."

After his meeting with Fabius Maximus, Scipio did not have much hope for the Roman government. Many of the women gathered were wives of the men attempting to keep Scipio from making ground toward what he saw as an obvious mode of

Roman victory. Laelius even spotted Fabius the Younger's wife among them.

Aemelia could see in her husband's expression that his cameo in the women's salon was distressing him, and announced that she had forgotten to mention an unbelievably impressive feat that her young Publius had performed. Scipio swiftly excused himself as the women changed subjects, and he and Laelius retired to the tablinum.

"You have to run," Laelius said. "There is no one else with the drive or the experience to take on the possession."

"But what if it's as Fabius the Younger said? What if I'm trapped in another political position where I cannot make any practical change?"

"These men served under your father," Laelius reminded him. "These are the men your father was leading, the men he talked about in all those letters he sent before his death. Those are the men who understand how important it is to take back Spain. You have to represent those men."

Scipio nodded. He looked thoughtful for a moment, and then stood to grab some paper and a writing utensil. He began to write vigorously.

Laelius sat and watched his friend. Back in the garden, he could see a few of the women curiously craning their necks to see what Scipio was up to.

On the day of the election, Scipio stood in the forum with the speech that he had written. At the other end of the forum was a tired, elderly consul named Brutus. He was the sacrificial lamb that Scipio's enemies in the senate had chosen so that Scipio would not simply win the position by default. As the sun rose high in the sky, Fabius Maximus, Fabius the Younger, and consuls representing the people's tribunes filed into the forum. One of the consuls announced the commencement of the election, detailed the position and its responsibility, and then acquiesced the floor to Scipio as the first candidate.

"Rome," Scipio began, "is a republic unlike any other. We are nestled in the heart of our motherland of Italy, but our reach stretches wide beyond her. At least, it did once." Fabius Maximus frowned as Scipio continued. "Many of you, like me, do not remember a Rome that was not at war. We do not remember the power of peace. Instead, we only know the strength of men who fought and who died defending this Republic, hoping one day we might find that peace again. My father and uncle and family for generations have been fighting to defend Rome. Many of you have similar histories as well. Yes, they fought for peace, but they also fought because they believed that Rome is unlike any other. We do a disservice to their legacy when doubting that Rome can rule over the lands in which these men fought in the name of Rome. We must continue to fight as they fought, and believe in the Rome in which they believed—in the Rome in which I believe!"

Scipio was predictably elected by a landslide, but his celebration was tainted by the knowledge that the senate would not allow him to reclaim the lands for which his father and uncle had fought so valiantly. Sitting in the garden at Villa Scipio, he held Aemelia's head in his lap and stroked her hair. Little Publius was studying a frog that had found its way into the pond at Vesta's feet. He clung to the statue's toes and lifted himself into a standing position, an act Publius had been prone to of late, which filled Scipio with the utmost pride. Aemelia was worried that the boy hadn't started to walk yet, but Scipio had only the highest regard for his son.

Laelius entered the garden and approached them.

Aemelia smiled. "Laelius told me that you wowed the consuls with your speech. I wish I could have been there to hear it," she said to Scipio, absentmindedly rubbing her engorged belly.

"You really were spectacular," Laelius agreed.

"Thank you both," Scipio sighed. He stood, kissed his wife, and put his hand on his friend's shoulder. "I will be doing my duty for the Roman people, even if it is in captivity."

A young aedile appeared at the doorway of the villa. "Proconsul," he said, "Fabius Maximus requests your audience immediately."

Scipio looked at Laelius, but only saw a mirror of his own perplexed expression. They bid Aemelia goodbye and headed off to the senate.

Scipio and Laelius reentered the small room off the main senate chambers in which they had previously met with Fabius Maximus. This time, Fabius Maximus was standing in the room completely alone. He asked Scipio and Laelius to sit before he began in a slow and careful manner.

"I was under the impression," Fabius Maximus said, "that I had been fully informed on the layout of Roman troops outside the city's walls, both in Italy and over in the Iberian Peninsula. Your speech, however, opened my eyes and caused me to question some of what I had previously considered to be true. Hannibal has been characterized in the hearts and minds of many Romans as a monster or a barbarian—even a vengeful god. But he is none of these. He is a smart, strategic foreign general. Given the rampant rumor and speculation that presently plague the city, it is sometimes difficult to remember that.

"Three of Hannibal's most experienced and trusted generals are operating throughout Spain as we speak: Mago, Hasdrubal Gisgo, and his brother, Hasdrubal Barca. For the past months, they have been bolstering Spanish tribes against Rome. When New Carthage was first established, I'd assumed it was simply a chauvinistically named resource depot, but now I see that there is more to it. If war is a game of numbers, then the Carthaginian generals in Spain are a much larger threat to Rome than a single general in Naples, infamous though he may be." Fabius Maximus sighed before continuing. He was not used to making decisive political plays. "What I am saying to you, Scipio, is that when you take up your role as proconsul in Spain, you have the Republic's permission to take the legion south of the Ebro, should you see fit."

Before Scipio could respond, Fabius Maximus added, "This is my decision, not the senate's. It is by my power as the leader of this country that I allow you to venture south. I trust you and I trust your expertise in the region. Do not disappoint me."

Scipio profusely thanked Fabius Maximus, who promptly dismissed him and Laelius. They spent the entire walk back to Villa Scipio excitedly discussing the plans they would set in motion once they arrived in Spain. Upon entering the house, they found a strange woman making an offering to the Vesta statue.

"Who are you?" Scipio inquired.

The woman turned and scoffed indignantly. She had seen enough ignorant husbands in her time and did not find them the least bit amusing.

"I'm the midwife, of course," she said.

Scipio's eyes widened. "Aemelia—"

"She's in here," the midwife said, leading him off to the master bedroom. "You haven't missed the baby yet."

Lucius Scipio, named for both of his uncles, was born on a warm spring evening just as the sun was setting. As his mother held him in her arms, his father stroked the thin hairs on his tiny round head. His eyes filled with tears of joy. Little Publius clung to his father's legs—he was just now learning how to walk. Scipio kissed his wife goodbye and swore to her that he would return. She knew it was a promise he could not keep, especially where he was going, but her heart nonetheless believed him. Scipio kissed his sons, turned to the door, and gave Laelius a nod. The two friends departed the house to begin the long journey to Spain.

Chapter Six

CROSSING THE EBRO—210 B.C.

The Spanish frontier bloomed brightly in the summer. Scipio looked out upon the rolling fields of green grass and wildflowers, which looked more like an artist's mural than reality. Emporiae was a small Roman base at the very edge of the Spanish frontier. The Tiber River had carried Scipio, as well as an army of eleven thousand, and a fleet of thirty quinquereme warships bestowed on him as proconsul, to the Roman stronghold. Now that they had made port, Scipio gathered his army and initiated the march toward the main Roman base at Tarraco, north of the Ebro River.

As the army neared Tarraco, Scipio and his men came upon a group of soldiers hunting hares.

"Brethren," Scipio shouted their way, "are you men of Publius the Elder's legion in Tarraco?"

The soldiers eyed Scipio and then shared a telling look. Laelius detected a great deal of suspicion.

One of the soldiers, an older veteran, finally stepped forward and spoke. "We were, but he was killed along with his brother. Now we pledge ourselves to Marcius."

"Marcius?" Laelius inquired.

"We elected him," a younger soldier in the group piped up. "He led us safely across the Ebro. We follow Marcius." His tone had become vaguely threatening.

No doubt they realized Scipio's identity. Sure enough the first soldier asked, "You're Scipio's son, then?"

Scipio nodded. The other soldiers grumbled among themselves, resembling wolves whose den had been disturbed by a more powerful pack. Scipio was evidently not wanted here.

The veteran cleared his throat, and in an effort to de-escalate the strained silence, said, "The base is a few miles west. You'll want to keep moving if you wish to arrive before the evening."

Scipio politely thanked the old soldier and directed the army to continue their march.

The environment in Tarraco was no less stressed. Upon their arrival, Scipio and Laelius witnessed a great deal of tension between the soldiers. They soon surmised that the base was suffering from a great schism. Despite reports of successful cooperation, Nero's men had never meaningfully integrated with the band that Marcius led north after Publius the Elder's defeat. Marcius told Scipio as much in the commander's tent.

"These men are fiercely loyal," Marcius explained. "Most of the men who survived the ambush at Castulo are combat veterans. They've been fighting for a long time and the allegiances they've made are difficult to sever."

Laelius did not trust a man who purported to be an innocent victim of his men's loyalty, but Scipio listened patiently.

Marcius sighed and took a seat. "I fought alongside these men. They elected me as their leader. They trust me. When Nero arrived, I tried to step down, but they wouldn't listen to Nero. They haven't fought with him, and the animosity has only escalated, and now that you're here with more men—"

"You're afraid it might be the spark that lights the fire," Scipio said. "But you and Nero are returning to the city."

"And I'm afraid that will only anger these men more," Marcius sighed again. "Your father instilled in them a fierce loyalty to the values of the Republic. They want their leaders to be their own elected representatives. They think that anything less is tantamount to tyranny." He chuckled wryly. "Your father was very effective."

"I can imagine," Scipio said sadly.

"We are holding a banquet tonight in honor of your arrival," Marcius informed him. "Perhaps we can find a way to gently introduce a transfer of power then without incurring too much protest."

Scipio thanked Marcius, and he and Laelius left the tent to ready themselves for the banquet.

"Do you trust him?" Laelius asked gravely.

"I trust that he will follow orders and transfer command to me," Scipio said. "I think Marcius is a good man who would like to help with the war, but sees Spain as a dead end. I'm sure he'll be happy to get back to Rome."

"And what about the men?" Laelius asked.

Scipio looked thoughtful for a moment. Laelius stopped him in the middle of the base and lowered his voice to a whisper.

"I think the only thing these men will respond to is intimidation. If they did not march in line for Nero, they obviously have no respect for the chain of command. I suggest you execute the first man who questions your authority as an example."

Scipio placed a hand on his friend's shoulder and flashed him a modest smile. "I don't think that will be necessary."

Scipio continued walking while Laelius eyed his back suspiciously. He had never known his friend to be so naïve.

The banquet began at the onset of twilight, and the three armies stationed at Tarraco sat in uncomfortably close proximity to one another beneath the gradually emerging stars. A great wooden table was placed at the head of the army. Marcius sat in the center chair flanked by Nero on his left and Scipio on his right. Once everyone's cups had been filled with wine, Marcius stood and lifted his goblet high. With the moon poking out from night clouds, Marcius began by thanking his men for the months of loyalty and diligent services they had given him.

"Many of us served under Publius the Elder or Gnaeus Scipio," he continued. "After they were betrayed and murdered at Castulo, we vowed to avenge their deaths and continue the fight they had begun." A cheer erupted from Marcius's men. "The leaders of our Republic have elected Publius the Elder's son to finish his father's work and lead Rome to victory. Though I may not be with you when you see the end of that fight, know that your victory will be mine because of the loyalty all of you have shown me. So, for all of us, I say, 'Fortuna!'"

A haphazard toast to Fortuna echoed through the armies. Many of the men mumbled gruffly among themselves, throwing shifty glances at Scipio.

A wide, courteous smile appeared on Scipio's face. He was seemingly unaware of the temperature of those gathered. He stood, holding his wine above his head.

"Thank you, Marcius. Thank you for your kind words toward my father and uncle, but you deny yourself. In leading these men, you have exhibited bravery the likes of which I have never seen in a commander." The mumblings quieted as the men listened intently. "After all, you carried many of these men to safety from an ambush that will go down in history as one of the most despicable. You fought your way past hostile Spanish tribes and unknown territory, showcasing your unmatched wisdom and courage."

A soldier near the back of the crowd whooped, sending a cheer rolling through the crowd like thunder.

Scipio continued, "Since your arrival in Tarraco, you have trained these men and led them with gravitas. My father and uncle would be proud to see where you've brought their men. Most of all," he added, "I am thankful that you have kept all these men together. In the city, it seems many things separate us—our houses, our vocations—but above all, we must remember that we are all Romans. We are one another's countrymen. These men elected you to lead them just as the men in the city elected me. I can only hope to follow in your brilliant example. So, for all of us, I say, 'To you, Marcius!'"

The crowd erupted into a deafening "Marcius!" Every soldier in the crowd sprang to his feet and gave Scipio a standing ovation. Scipio merely stood before them with an air of humility.

That night, the new proconsul met with Nero and Marcius in the commander's tent.

"That was quite a speech you made," Nero commented. "You have a talent for winning over difficult crowds."

"But we wanted to caution you that, even with a united front, you won't find this region easily subdued," Marcius warned.

Scipio looked at him quizzically.

Marcius cleared his throat. "That is, Nero and I wanted to make abundantly clear to you the forces that face Rome in Spain."

Scipio leaned forward. He had been waiting for precisely this.

"It is no secret that your purpose in Spain is to march southward onto New Carthage," Nero said.

Scipio began to speak, but Nero held up his hand. "We do not want to discourage you, but rather warn you that such an advance may not be as simple as you think."

"As I'm sure you are aware, either from official correspondence or communication with your father, we had a great many allies among the Spanish tribes," Marcius explained. "That all changed after Castulo. Every Spanish kingdom south of the Ebro River is hostile to us and under Carthage's control. However, their allegiance to Carthage is incredibly strained. Hasdrubal Barca, Hasdrubal Gisgo, and Mago all maintain the Spanish kings' loyalty through intimidation. Their men ride throughout the south of Spain committing horrific acts of violence and oppression against the Spanish tribes to maintain control. They take hostages, burn down entire villages, and occupy townships with men. The kings are afraid and so they attack us with fear, not true loyalty to Carthage.

"The key to a victory against New Carthage," Marcius went on, "is to reclaim and expand those alliances with Spanish tribes. Roman troops won't be able to get close to the gates of the city without their support, and even if they take New Carthage, the army will be surrounded by enemy forces. The most powerful tribe is the Edetani, who are led by an ancient Iberian bloodline. Most of the other tribes follow their example, and if any of the tribes contest you, it will be paramount to have them on your side."

Scipio recalled his father mentioning the Edetani as important Spanish allies.

"The Spanish tribes are not all that lie between here and New Carthage," Nero said, picking up where Marcius left off. "The three Carthaginian generals have stationed their forces across the country. At least one army will be in close enough proximity to New Carthage to run to its aid if it is attacked. If you do not engage with the Carthaginians before you arrive at New Carthage, you will certainly draw them back to the city by laying siege."

"They communicate incredibly well," Marcius added. "Battling with one army is like attacking a lion's single paw: There are three more and a head of terrible teeth that will come to its defense."

"And the city has its own army and fortifications," Nero continued. "We have spies on the outside surveying the city, and they have confirmed that the defensive forces within the city are no small matter. The city itself is encircled by a huge stone wall with a moat surrounding it. Even given the manpower of our three forces combined, the loss of life during a siege would be tremendous."

"All of this to say," Marcius concluded, "that the campaign you propose to run is dangerous, and much of it is in the hands of Fortuna. Gaining allies will be the only way to carry out an attack on New Carthage, and the Carthaginians know it, so be very careful whom you trust. Trust is what cost your father and uncle their lives."

"Marcius," Nero interjected, "it is time we depart."

Nero rose from his seat. Marcius nodded and stood as well.

"Fortuna, General Scipio," Marcius said.

Scipio nodded. The three men saluted one another before Marcius and Nero left the tent to commence their journey back to Rome.

Laelius, who, as always, had been quietly and intently listening, approached Scipio. "Well, they are certainly more receptive to the idea of a siege on New Carthage than the consuls in Rome. From what they were saying, it seems like the most difficult part of a campaign would be invading New Carthage without engaging one of the Carthaginian armies."

"Exactly. That is why we are going to engage all three," Scipio informed him.

Laelius stared at Scipio. Had he lost his mind? Attack Hannibal's three most skilled generals? Was he insane?

Scipio gestured for Laelius to sit down, and outlined his strategy. "My plan was actually never to take New Carthage. Doing so would give us no strategic advantage, only a symbolic victory. As Marcius just outlined, the city is well fortified, and an ongoing siege would cost us time, resources, and men. Meanwhile, any of the three Carthaginian armies could come attack us from the other side at any moment. Furthermore, and this is the piece that neither Nero nor Marcius nor any other consul seems to consider, Hannibal will still be in Naples. If we attack Carthage's European capital, there is a good chance he will retaliate by attacking Rome, and Rome will be worse off than it was before. However, given the armies and resources we possess in Tarraco right now, we should be able to take on all three of the Carthaginian armies. It's just as Marcius said: If we attack one paw, the rest of the beast will come to its defense. That is what we are betting on."

"But I thought Nero said that we would not be able to take on all three armies," Laelius clarified.

"Not if we're also using men and resources to attack the city," Scipio explained. "But if we only pretend to attack the city, and then turn around and attack the armies with our full force, we outnumber our enemies. A defeat that large would have to draw Hannibal out of Italy to defend New Carthage and avenge the defeat of not one but *three* of his best generals."

Laelius was beginning to see the plan unfold before him. He was stunned by Scipio's innovation.

"But what if something were to go wrong? What if the forces in New Carthage attack us from behind or it isn't as Marcius says and the three armies do not battle all at once?" Laelius asked.

"That is why I need you at the head of the naval fleet," Scipio said, his tone excited but dire. "As Nero mentioned, there is a moat surrounding New Carthage. The moat empties into the sea. I need you to station the naval fleet at the edge of the moat. Should anything go wrong, or if we should be ambushed on land like my father and uncle, our army will escape by sea."

Laelius agreed to the task, telling Scipio that it would be an honor.

Scipio gripped Laelius's arm tightly, looking into his eyes gravely. "Laelius, it is of tantamount importance that no one else knows my true intentions. If word gets out that we are not planning a siege of New Carthage, then any hope of ambushing all three Carthaginian armies at once is dashed."

Laelius told Scipio that he understood and would tell no one else of the true plan.

After Scipio's rousing speech at the banquet, the climate of the base changed almost overnight. Scipio's and Nero's men began to quickly integrate with Marcius's. Over the next few weeks, as Scipio prepared his men to march south of the Ebro, the men came to trust Scipio more and more. Those who had known his father saw his potential as a similar leader. Even his youth began to appear as an asset to the older veterans, most of whom had participated in enough combat not to mistake age for wisdom. Scipio was, on many accounts, the most informed and studious commander the men had ever served.

As Scipio's popularity soared among his men, the army also caught wind of whisperings from local Spanish merchants and villagers that Scipio was planning to attack New Carthage. The rumors played perfectly into Scipio's plan. Not only did the prospect of action against the Carthaginians excite the army and further ally them to Scipio, but such rumors would also draw the Carthaginian armies to him, just as Scipio hoped. His entire strategy banked on the Carthaginians attacking in one, unified force.

As Scipio prepared his men to march, Laelius readied the naval fleet to sail down the coast of Spain as backup. He would try to remain as close to shore and in line with Scipio's army as possible without drawing attention to the fleet. The fleet's secrecy was paramount, which Laelius stressed to his men. Should the Carthaginians spot them first, they would be attacked without the manpower of Scipio's army to protect them. Laelius planned to set sail directly after Scipio's army began their march.

The night before Scipio was set to cross the Ebro, he and Laelius reiterated their plan.

"Should anything out of the ordinary happen," Laelius emphasized, "the fleet will be able to carry you and the army back to Tarraco." Laelius sensed hesitation in his friend's eyes. "Will you make that call, Scipio?"

Scipio was silent.

Laelius prodded, "I know the last thing you want to do is retreat back to the north, but Tarraco is the safest, most secure base Rome has in the region. Even if you make friends with the Edetani and the other Spanish kings, the best place to regroup will be back here. I know you don't want to lose the land, but—"

Scipio stopped him. He looked into his eyes and confirmed, "I'll make the call, Laelius, if necessary."

An older Spanish man appeared in the entryway to the tent. By the look of his dress and the weight of travel on his brow, Laelius deduced that he must be a merchant. Beside him stood a veteran solider who had been in Marcius's legion.

"Commander," the soldier said, "this man is one of our allies from the area surrounding New Carthage. He claims to have important information."

Scipio gestured for the merchant to enter, then dismissed the soldier. "You must have traveled a long way," he said.

The merchant nodded. "We have heard that you are planning an attack on New Carthage," he ventured.

"What information do you have?" Scipio inquired, noncommittal.

The merchant sighed. "My family has lived in the region on the outskirts of the city for generations. We depend on that land to make food, to keep a house—to live! The city has completely altered the environment. It has devastated the flora and fauna in the area. The land is utterly changed. The Carthaginians came in with a complete ignorance and disregard for the environment and, as a result, the establishment of their city ravaged it. Worst of all is the moat that they built around the gates—"

"I imagine that the appearance of a large trench of water would alter some things," Scipio conceded, somewhat impatiently.

"But that's just it!" the merchant exclaimed. "They had no idea what they were doing when they built that moat, especially how severe the low tide is. The moat is shallow. It may not seem so to the untrained eye, but at low tide, it can be forded on foot. Your knees wouldn't feel a splash!"

Scipio took this all in. "Why are you telling us this now?"

The merchant looked self-conscious. "I was under the impression that Rome no longer had any interest in those of us so far south. You've been north of the Ebro for a while now. But then I heard word of your plan to attack the city and my faith was reinvigorated."

"Thank you, sir. You have helped us tremendously."

The merchant offered a small bow and departed.

"Should we tell the other men about this?" Laelius asked.

Scipio thoughtfully shook his head. "For now, we will stick to the plan."

"But wouldn't it be helpful to know that we can use the moat—"

Scipio shot Laelius a knowing look. It was the same look that Scipio always had when he had formed a plan.

"The information will become clear in due time," he assured Laelius.

The next morning, Scipio gathered his generals, infantry, and cavalry together. They all stood in perfect formation on the north side of the Ebro River. The vast fields of the Spanish frontier had greened with the nearing of the summer solstice. The sun was bright. The air buzzed with promise and anticipation. Laelius stood off from the rest, ready to depart with Scipio's fleet as soon as the march began.

Scipio took his place at the front of the army. In a single, valiant motion, he signaled his men and began to cross the Ebro.

Chapter Seven

NEPTUNE'S BLESSING—209 B.C.

Laelius set sail from Tarraco into calm waters. He had never before ventured out onto the vast Mediterranean Sea. He could not help but be awed by the infinite horizon at the edge of the waves. At first it looked to him like a new frontier, the emerald waves reminiscent of the green fields of the Iberian Peninsula in the distance, swaying synchronously with the wind and forming beautiful patterns in their undulations. But the more time Laelius spent looking out from the deck of his ship, the more he realized that the waves were more mountains than fields, rising to incredible heights and crashing back down or fading quietly into untroubled water.

As was the custom, the fleet asked for Neptune's blessing before setting sail, and now that they'd been some weeks at sea, Laelius was grateful they had. Playing at naval commander in the Roman marketplace had in no way prepared him for the real thing. Though their travels had been relatively mild, a summer storm had hit a few days back and shaken parts of the fleet, most notably their commander. Laelius had emptied his stomach overboard multiple times over the last few days. He swore to himself that he would never underestimate the power of Neptune.

Laelius had received little word from Scipio since the two commenced their separate commands within the campaign. From what he could tell, they were still in line with Scipio's army, which meant that the legion was progressing smoothly. Every nautical message that the fleet received from the coast amounted to "stay the course." Evidently, none of the Spanish tribes who had pledged their loyalty to Carthage was moved to stop the southward march.

Laelius also learned that command of a naval fleet was much quieter than command of the army. He left most of the guidance and navigation up to his captains, spending time building up the men's spirits. Even this, however, left Laelius with a great deal of time to think and reflect.

One night, staring into the twirling cosmos and glittering starlight from the deck of his ship, Laelius recalled a conversation he had witnessed between Scipio and his father years ago. It must, he thought, have been during that first winter he spent at Villa Scipio. He remembered a dinner they had enjoyed, a deliciously prepared garum fish sauce with fresh slices of olive bread. Scipio and his father had gotten into a debate about the larger implications of the war. Though Laelius could not recall exactly what recent news had sparked the discussion, he remembered it had spurred Publius the Elder to think back to his role in the First War.

"But the First War was fought in Sicily," Scipio insisted. "Now Carthage has crossed the sea and Hannibal's army has come over the Alps into Italy. His generals in Spain are terrorizing

European people. They established a capital city on the European mainland. Isn't that the most pressing issue?"

"We never thought that Carthage would extend itself beyond the Mediterranean," Scipio's father sighed. There was a hint of disappointment in his voice. "During the First War, we were sure of so many things. We were sure that our army would easily do away with the force of the small Phoenician principality. We were wrong. We thought building a fleet would tip the odds in our favor. Again, we were wrong. We thought that Sicily and Corsica's proximity to Rome, that the Italian people living in those islands, and their loyalty to Rome, would win us the day against Carthage. Instead, we settled for a stalemate in Sicily, exhausting all of our resources and our soldiers."

Publius the Elder slurped some of his garum while Scipio's mother brought out dates for dessert.

"Another thing we were sure of," Publius the Elder said, "was the fight was not over. We were right about that. But we never would have imagined that Carthage would go as far as set foot on the mainland of Europe. Now, not only are they here, but they occupy both Spain and Italy. As you said, they have a capital city on European land."

"So, why don't you think ousting Carthage from Europe is the best thing Rome can do to win the war?" Scipio asked.

"Because doing so will not win us the war," Publius the Elder concluded, pounding his fork down on the table. "Your uncle has been fighting the Carthaginians in Spain, and I in Italy, beating back foreign armies who have taken over more territory than Sicily and Corsica combined. But both of us acknowledge that the battles we are fighting are a temporary fix, because as soon as Carthage is thrown off the mainland, they will escalate. That is the nature of this war. That is how Hannibal and the

Carthaginians fight. They escalate." Publius the Elder had raised slightly from his seat, inflated with passion. He sat down and resumed his imposing and dignified posture. "Carthage will not stop conquering as long as their capital still stands in Africa."

Laelius remembered Scipio internalizing his father's conclusion after dinner that night in the garden.

"Do you really think a general would ever do what your father is suggesting?" Laelius asked. "Would somebody really sail an army over to Africa and try to take the Carthaginian capital?"

Scipio was thoughtful for a minute and then shook his head. "A Roman general would never be able to do it alone. Carthage would have him surrounded immediately. Even with Carthage out of Europe, he would need the collective support of every kingdom and principality in North Africa. Besides, my father is having enough difficulty convincing Fabius Maximus and the other consuls to look beyond the Italian Peninsula. The government is way too defensive to sanction a campaign to Africa." He exhaled and tilted his head upward, gazing into an indigo, star-dappled sky much like the one Laelius viewed from the deck of his ship.

"Then again," Scipio had added, "as my father said, they were sure of so many things before Hannibal crossed the Alps."

After a novel and not-terribly-pleasant maiden voyage, Laelius spotted the wall of New Carthage sandy-white atop the Spanish palisades. The fleet approached the inlet that fed into the lagoon connecting New Carthage's moat to the Mediterranean. Laelius instructed the fleet to pause by the hills out of sight until twilight to utilize the darkness while maintaining enough light to safely navigate the rocky shoals of the lagoon.

That evening, as the sunset faded into a silvery-violet twilight, Laelius's fleet sailed inconspicuously into the lagoon. They came to a safe distance from the walls of the city, far enough that a sentry atop the wall would not distinguish them from harmless merchant ships, and moored the fleet in the lagoon. Then, Laelius simply waited to hear from Scipio.

When a Roman messenger finally arrived with word from Scipio, the message was so unbelievable that Laelius almost wondered if it might be a forgery: They were to go ahead with a siege of the city! Despite the Romans' nearly uninterrupted campaign from Tarraco to the gates of New Carthage, the Carthaginian generals had not responded or made any signs of engaging with Scipio's army. Frustrated by his miscalculation, Scipio concluded that the only way to attract their attention would be to go through with an attack on the city. According to the message, the siege would begin at dawn, and Laelius would attack the south side of the city with the full force of the navy. Of course, no one else was shocked by this news, as they had thought that a siege had been the plan from the beginning. A few of his generals were perplexed at Laelius's reaction to what appeared to be a routine command. Nevertheless, Laelius prepared his men for battle to commence the following morning.

At first light, Scipio stood at the edge of the moat that circumnavigated New Carthage. He noted that the moat did appear incredibly deep. Then again, the tide had not yet receded. His army was poised behind him. He had received confirmation from Laelius the night before that his fleet had arrived and were ready as well. Scipio watched the waves lap at the sandy bank. Soon, he realized the bank was growing. He thrust his sword into the air, as if to slice the pale blue morning sky.

"Neptune," Scipio announced, "ruler and protector of the seas and waves and water, give us your blessing that we may reign victorious over the Carthaginians, who with their garish city pretend to conquer your domain. Bestow upon us your might and courage!"

Those at the front of the company gasped as the water swiftly slunk away from Scipio's feet. Others tried to muscle their way in for a view. Though few men could truthfully say that they saw the waves recede at Scipio's whim, the meaning was clear: Neptune had given the Roman army his blessing. With an ear-splitting shout, the men charged across the shallow moat. Their knees barely felt a splash.

From his ship at the head of the fleet, Laelius had also seen the moat recede. Thankfully, he had moored the ships just at the edge of the lagoon where the water was still suitably deep. However, even from a distance, Scipio's banishment of the water seemed like a miracle to the other soldiers on the ship. Only Laelius knew—and would ever know—that the true blessing came from an old Spanish merchant.

Scipio's army immediately began to scale the walls of the city. The garrison defending the city was led by a general named Mago, not to be confused with the Carthaginian general whose attention Scipio had been trying to attract. This Mago was, in fact, stationed in the city because he had very little talent for fighting. He excelled in the everyday subjugation of upstart Spanish peasants as well as the many hostages and political prisoners they were housing within New Carthage's walls. However, when Mago received word that Roman troops had propped ladders on the north end of the city's wall and were steadily on their way inside, he knew that the end of his command had come.

Scipio's men were as surprised as New Carthage's defense. Laying siege to Carthage's main port and most important territory in Europe proved incredibly easy. Roman soldiers started to surge over the top of the north wall with little resistance. An insignificant collection of Mago's forces gathered at the top of the wall, throwing rocks and shooting arrows down onto the intruders, but to little effect. The first soldiers to make it over the wall immediately began cutting them down.

Laelius's men made their way over the wall as well. Leaving the ships in the hands of the naval captains, Laelius led a majority of the soldiers who had sailed with him up the south end of the hill. Like their counterparts on the opposite end of the city, they too proceeded by first propping immense ladders against the sandstone wall. They then swiftly began to climb the ladders. When Laelius was nearly halfway to the peak, a small shadow appeared against the bright morning clouds. Shortly after, Laelius saw a large stone speeding toward him. He gave a shout and hugged the ladder. The stone hit the ladder, shaking the men, but it remained intact. Laelius gave another shout and they ascended the ladders faster. His arms and knees burned with exertion, uninterrupted except for pauses taken to avoid a few more descending projectiles. But in no time Laelius was over the wall, sword in hand. As soon as his feet hit stone, he began slashing at the sentries. However, he quickly realized that the defense on the wall was sparse.

From the ground, Scipio could not make sense of the action atop the wall, and at first refused to believe that New Carthage would be left so lightly defended. Scipio started to put together a contingency plan in case an unaccounted-for garrison were to appear to defend the city. However, Scipio discarded that possibility when he noticed a legion of Carthaginian soldiers marching out of the city led by Mago. They were retreating! Scipio sent a group of soldiers to intercept them, but his excitement clouded his mind. Butterflies fluttered optimistically in his stomach. Minutes later, the gates of New Carthage opened, and

Scipio marched in. Carthage's European capital was conquered within hours.

Though the Romans had taken the city speedily, the aftermath of the siege was far from simple. Mago had regrouped his forces at a nearby Carthaginian camp. The group that Scipio had initially sent after them was unable to take the garrison, so Scipio had sent reinforcements. Meanwhile, he was faced with what to do with the Carthaginian city. His first act was freeing every hostage housed there. He also directed his troops to drain all surplus resources in the city's stores. New Carthage was also home to Carthage's war treasury, which he also promptly emptied.

Scipio's most pressing concern was feuding that had sprung up among the men.

"They both want the *corona muralis*," Laelius informed Scipio.

For days after the initial siege, Scipio's army and Laelius's naval force had been arguing which group deserved the award. The corona muralis was given to the first party to breech the wall, but because the city had been taken so quickly from both sides, it was difficult to tell which force merited the recognition. Personally, Scipio found such awards trivial, but he knew that it meant a great deal to many of the men under his command.

"And you have no clue when you made it to the top of the wall?" Scipio asked Laelius.

Laelius shook his head. "All of us acted on your command. The whole siege happened so quickly, I didn't have time to register where your men where."

Suddenly, a soldier appeared in the doorway. "General

Scipio," the young infantryman said in earnest, "some men have set fire to one of the apartment buildings."

Scipio and Laelius ran to the window. Sure enough, smoke was rising from a few blocks away.

Scipio spun and confronted the infantryman. "Who did this?"

"It was a group of naval officers, sir."

Laelius stiffened. It was his men.

Scipio eyed the soldier suspiciously. "Was there any reason why the naval officers set fire to the apartments?"

The soldier shifted uncomfortably. He was very young, with boyish features that don't fade long into a man's second decade, and likely was not used to being stared down by an eminent general. He cracked.

"A group of soldiers that were part of the land forces raided a nobleman's house last night. You see, they were arguing with the naval officers about who should get the corona muralis, and the soldiers said that they were clearly the more powerful invaders and the naval officers dared them to prove it, so—"

"Would you say the situation has escalated?" Scipio interrupted gruffly. The soldier nodded. "Tell them that their commander demands they extinguish the fire immediately."

The soldier nodded and moved to leave, but Scipio was not finished.

"Tell them also that I do not appreciate men who report misconduct with malicious intent against their fellow Romans." Scipio shot a telling look directly into the soldier's eyes. He might have become a puddle on the spot. "We are one army, after all."

The soldier ran off and, within minutes, the smoke in the distance died down. However, over the coming days, Scipio continued to receive tips that factions of the naval and land forces were raiding and destroying Carthaginian property. Still, he did not assign either side the corona muralis.

"If you don't care about the award, then why not just assign it to someone?" Laelius asked him.

Scipio contemplatively stroked his smooth chin, sitting in a gold-rimmed chair that had belonged to Mago. The lamplight flickered in the gold lining, bringing it to life.

"That wouldn't be right," Scipio said wearily. "I may not care for the award, but I won't just give it away."

"Then what do you propose to do? An execution or some other kind of disciplinary action coming from you would definitely end the destruction, but it could also antagonize the men, and these men are mean. I don't know if it's because they were expecting more of a fight during the siege or if it's that this is their first real chance to hit back at Carthage for all the suffering it has caused Rome, but they're out for blood. If you do nothing, these men will level the city."

Scipio's brow furrowed as he stared out into the cloudy night. Another fire had been set in what looked like the central square of the city. The surrounding structures were grotesquely orange against the serene starless night. Laelius found some weariness in the corners of Scipio's eyes. Mago's garrison had still not surrendered, and Scipio wanted to aim as much effort as he could at quashing his forces once and for all. Until he did, his siege would feel incomplete. Though he had taken the city, he still did not feel victorious.

"What if we let them?" Scipio finally said.

"Let them what?"

"Let them level the city?" Scipio asked.

Laelius stared at Scipio in disbelief.

Scipio stood and squarely faced his friend. "I never wanted

to lay siege to the city. In the original plan, the city is better as ash than in Carthaginian hands."

"But the plan has changed."

"Of course! But my goals have not. The plan was to engage the Carthaginian generals in Spain. That still has not happened. Obviously, Hannibal's generals must not think that occupying New Carthage is threatening enough. If we stay in this city, we are taking a defensive stance and giving up the offensive. But if we let these men destroy the city, they will be destroying the symbol of Carthage's presence in Spain. It will send a message that Mago, Hasdrubal Barca, and Hasdrubal Gisgo will be unable to ignore."

"And what about the people here?" Laelius asked. "Are we going to let these men massacre them?"

Scipio considered this. "Take the Carthaginians still residing in the city as prisoners," he said. "But let all the Spaniards go home. They will tell their villages and tribes and noblemen and kings of the power that Rome has shown over Carthage."

Two days later, Scipio and Laelius stood side by side at the outer rim of New Carthage's moat. They listened to the crash and rumble of the buildings falling to rubble. When the men had gotten word to destroy the city, the corona muralis was forgotten. Laelius was correct: They were out for blood. The feuding had simply been an avenue through which the men could express their hatred, and hatred joined them together once again. If they were honest with themselves, Laelius and Scipio too felt the uplifting satisfaction of vengeance. Scipio's army toppled the Carthaginian capital like waves washing away a sandcastle.

Those less destructive soldiers helped usher the remaining citizens out of the city, either to join the camp as prisoners or return to their homes, depending on their nationality. The world had flipped on its head for many of them over the past weeks, and whatever lay ahead was uncertain for all. A soldier ran up to Scipio and informed him that Mago's garrison had finally surrendered. After all, what had they to defend now that the city was crumbling?

Laelius admired Scipio as he gazed proudly into the setting sun. Victory was theirs.

Chapter Eight

BATTLE AT BAECULA—208 B.C.

Word spread quickly of Scipio's lethal blow to New Carthage. It traveled up through the Spanish tribes and kingdoms, across the Alps and northern principalities, and landed in Rome, buzzing throughout the city. Scipio's actions at New Carthage were lauded as the first Roman victory in years. The city exploded with even more excitement when Mago arrived in Rome as a prisoner and spoil of war. The Roman Senate attempted to take credit for the siege, claiming it was a collaborative effort between Scipio and the other consuls. However, Scipio was undeniably admired as the hero. In case the military wasn't enough, Aemelia made sure that Roman society was aware of her husband's courage.

Having returned to the military base in Tarraco, Scipio continued to sort through the materials, supplies, resources, and provisions that his army had gained from New Carthage. It seemed that the Carthaginians had heavily overstocked the city. Because New Carthage had been their main port in Europe, the Carthaginians had filled it with fruits, grains, vegetation, metalwork, precious stones, and strategic plans that would have quickly and easily been transported between the two continents. Numidian horses, African flora, and special forms of iron only found in northern Africa were just a few prizes that the Romans took home with them as they crossed north of the Ebro. This crossing was not tainted by mourning or apprehension, but instead was filled with celebration.

The gain that Scipio prized most was the newfound respect that the Spanish tribes offered the Romans. Though Scipio's campaign southward had been largely undisturbed by the locals, every step of their return to Tarraco was met with cheers and blessings. The Spanish villagers honored Scipio and praised his destruction of the symbol of Carthage's occupation. They pledged their loyalty to Rome, offering up food and lodging for the army.

Scipio could not help but think of the old merchant who had informed him of the shallow moat. He would mention him to Laelius once in a while after their return to Tarraco. The Carthaginians had come and destroyed the homes of countless Spanish who had lived on the land for generations. It was no wonder the Spanish rejoiced at their invaders' defeat.

As winter fell and Scipio's army settled back at Tarraco, Scipio continued to liaise with local Spanish tribes and win their trust. Not long after the army had secured itself for the winter, Edeco, an Edetani prince, arrived and asked for an audience with the commander. Edeco was the descendant of an ancient bloodline of Spanish royalty who had ruled the region between the Ebro and Sucro rivers for generations. Scipio immediately accepted his request, and they met in the commander's tent. Scipio had purposely crowded it with spoils from New Carthage as décor. Laelius observed as the prince's eyes fell over every precious object, obviously impressed.

Edeco had swarthy olive skin, wavy dark brown hair, and soulful copper eyes. He had the mouth of a man who was often displeased, always felt superior, but also laughed at joyful things. He had the appearance of royalty, which added to Scipio and Laelius's shock when the young prince took to his knees.

"General Scipio," Edeco said, his eyes fixed on the floor, "you are in possession of some things very dear to me."

"And what are those?" Scipio asked. It was not often that he was completely lost in a situation.

"My wife and children were kidnapped and held as ransom in New Carthage. I have not seen or spoken to them in years. I would like nothing more than to have them returned to me. In exchange, I will vow my family's allegiance to you and your cause."

Scipio, though confused, caught on quickly. He immediately sent for Edeco's family to be found among the prisoners and brought to the tent.

He turned back and gently told the prince, "I apologize for a grave mistake. The Spanish prisoners were supposed to be released, but my men must have confused your wife and children for Carthaginians. Rest assured that they have not been harmed. They will be here soon."

When Edeco's family entered the tent, they immediately rushed to him. They all fell to the floor with overtures of grateful sobs and kisses, and wrapped in a tight embrace.

"I have a wife and two sons myself," Scipio interjected. "I could not imagine my family being taken from me with such despicable intentions."

"Thank you," Edeco replied, tears still in his eyes. "Consider the Edetani a loyal friend to Rome and to Scipio until the end of time."

Overjoyed to have been reunited, the prince and his family departed for their home. Laelius marveled at Fortuna, and smiled at Scipio.

"The Edetani are the most powerful allies you could gain in Spain," Laelius commented.

Scipio nodded. "With Edeco pledged to Rome, the rest of the Spanish kingdoms will follow suit. That means that this spring, we'll march south again."

"To take on the three generals?" Laelius inquired.

Scipio nodded gravely. Even throughout the winter, more reports of the Carthaginian armies terrorizing Spanish villages had reached Scipio. It was time to end Carthage's presence in Spain in totality.

"With Edeco, we will not lose," Scipio muttered.

But the season was not kind to Scipio's men. Many of his company came down with severe pneumonia, while others suffered from food poisoning. Though the casualties during the siege at New Carthage had been manageable, the winter did away with a large fraction of Scipio's army. As the dewy first flowers of spring emerged from the winter-chapped fields, Scipio realized that his forces would no longer be able to take on all three Carthaginian armies.

"We'll have to take them on one at a time," Scipio confided in Laelius.

His friend agreed. Though they had lost many men, time was of the essence, and still they had the Edetani and their allies on their side.

As spring swiftly thawed the Spanish frontier, Scipio called upon Edeco to bring more neighboring Spanish kingdoms into Rome's ranks. Not a week later, Indibilis, one of Spain's most influential chieftains, arrived at Tarraco to discuss pledging his allegiance to Rome. The more tribes that defected over to Rome's side, the more Scipio's confidence grew.

Meanwhile, Scipio also set about training his army and readying them for battle. After Cannae, he had studied the Carthaginian army's tactics every time he confronted them. The image of the Roman infantry bursting apart so suddenly still played in his mind. The typical Roman infantry formation had been developed to engage with other organized infantry formations. However, Carthage's infantry of Spanish and Celtic warriors took advantage of the infantry's predictability and shattered the center of the infantry every time.

Over the years, Scipio had been developing a new formation in which he would train his army. He created a novel military position known as a cohort. The cohorts, supported by the cavalry, would stop the enemy from rushing the infantry and breaking the formation as they usually did. It would also expand the area of the infantry to prevent enemy tribes from ambushing them as easily. Scipio spent the first weeks of spring integrating the cohorts into his infantry.

When the spring showers had fully washed away the winter, Scipio strategized with Edeco and his other newfound Spanish allies. They discussed how best to go about taking the three armies down, one by one. Marcius's concern over the armies' advanced communication and coordination was echoed in the tribal leaders. Word reached them that Hasdrubal Barca had camped his army near Baecula, the location of the last silver mines still under Carthaginian control.

"It's one of the most strategic locations for Hasdrubal to

station his army," Indibilis cautioned. "An offensive on any army stationed there would mean fighting twice as hard to gain any progress."

"But Baecula is also directly blocking the road southward," Edeco argued. "It will be impossible to advance south without engaging the army."

"Then that is what we will do," Scipio said. "The spring is here. It is time we begin the campaign. Should we skirmish with Hasdrubal, I am confident that we will succeed."

The air was filled with the scent of fresh poppies and geraniums. Scipio's army marched past patches of newly bloomed Spanish bluebells as they moved deliberately south, though they were cautious. They were in the heart of Carthaginian Spain. Even with the conquering of New Carthage and the defection of the Edetani to Scipio's side, Carthage had a tight hold on many tribes. Scipio's army had no friends here. They tried their best to avoid the main roads and towns, depending on their own stores for food and water. The men did not trust the few travelers and farmers they met along the way.

Scipio marched at the head of his army—he insisted upon it—with Laelius by his side. He insisted upon that as well. Scipio had crossed the Ebro River with more reserve than he had the first time. He was shrewd enough to know that Fortuna would not bless them with the luck that they had found at New Carthage. Hasdrubal's men were trained by one of Carthage's greatest generals, second only to Hannibal, and these fiercely loyal fighters had honed their skills and aggression through years of occupation on the Iberian Peninsula. Scipio had the utmost confidence in his men and his strategy, but he was not a fool.

After his siege of New Carthage, many in Rome and throughout his army had lauded him as one of history's greatest generals. But his father and uncle had been called "great" as well, and they had perished in Spain. He wondered if he would suffer a similar fate.

In fact, he thought about his father and uncle's deaths quite often after Edeco had approached him. Both Scipio patriarchs had met their demise by placing their trust in the wrong allies. Scipio trusted Edeco's allegiance, as he had seen the man's desperation and elation at having his family returned to him firsthand. Furthermore, Edeco appeared to be a man of his word, concerned with leaving a positive legacy and upholding his family's ancient name. Indibilis also appeared trustworthy, though he had no expressed reason for allying with Rome besides a hatred of Carthage. Scipio was more suspicious of his brother, Mandonius, who seemed as tense as a cat at any mention of Rome.

While Scipio agreed to ally with these Spanish princes and took their counsel, he held onto a great deal of distrust. He had all their suggestions double-checked by Roman scouts, and refused to break bread with them. He did not reveal his suspicions of their Spanish allies to Laelius until much later. He told himself it was to help maintain the alliances without the risk of his distrust being publicized, but deep down he knew that Laelius would never tell. He was afraid, and trust is difficult to nurture in the face of fear.

Scipio's army camped near the Guadalquivir River in the Baetis Valley, just a few miles from Hasdrubal's camp at Baecula. Scipio had set up camp to intercept anyone entering the valley. As there was no sign of Hasdrubal leaving his defensive location at Baecula, Scipio would camp there for a few weeks and continue training his army while choking Hasdrubal's army from one side. Scipio and Edeco were in the commander's tent finalizing their plans for training when a soldier rushed in.

"We intercepted a messenger trying to sneak past us on the river," he said. "His message was that Mago and Hasdrubal Gisgo are expected to join Hasdrubal Barca in three days' time."

"Three?!" Edeco exclaimed, jumping to his feet. "Three days? That isn't nearly enough time to organize our armies. We still have weeks of training scheduled."

"But do we have the resources or the manpower to attack all three armies? We would have to scrap our current formations and create a completely new one that would only stretch us thinner," Laelius reminded Edeco.

They both looked to Scipio, whose brow had grown heavy with concern. The right side of his mouth twitched. Finally, he spoke, "Tell the men we will begin our offensive in two days."

Edeco nodded anxiously, flashing Laelius a desperate look before exiting the tent.

"We'll do as much preparation over the next two days as possible. We've been training well," Scipio reassured Laelius. "We will still defeat Hasdrubal Barca's army."

Two days later, Scipio's forces stood at the tempestuous waters of the Guadalquivir. Recent rains had engorged the river, which now flooded the banks and ran swiftly past the Roman army. Hasdrubal's camp lay at the top of the imposing, tree-spotted hill that stretched before them. Scipio's legions were beginning their attack at a disadvantage by advancing from lower ground, which is why Hasdrubal chose to build his camp where he had. However, Scipio hoped they had the element of surprise on their side. The Carthaginians had likely spotted the Roman camp being built two days ago, and Hasdrubal would not expect them to attack in such a short amount of time.

The past two days had been taxing, particularly on Scipio. He had studied weeks' worth of training and had to choose the most important tactics in which to train and refresh his army without exhausting his men. Scipio had not slept for nearly forty-eight hours. But watching the overflowing river run past, he felt emboldened by the rushing water. He let the crash and suck of the powerful waves revitalize him. Looking downstream of the river, he saw Laelius poised at the ready with the other half of Scipio's command. Splitting the army had been Laelius's idea—that a double offensive would increase their chances of surprising the Carthaginians and allow the Romans to ambush them. Scipio silently gave the signal, and the two halves began to cross the river and ascend the hill on either side.

The Roman army made it farther up the hill than either Scipio or Laelius had expected. In fact, those at the front of the legions could barely glimpse the training exercises of the enemy that were interrupted when a lookout announced the army's approach. Like a terrifying conglomerate beast, Hasdrubal's army moved into position against Scipio's. They began to rain stones down upon the advancing Romans. Laelius gave a shout and his men lifted their shields above their heads. The thud of stones hitting metal rang throughout the air, warning Scipio's half just in time for them to raise their shields before a barrage of stones fell on their side as well. They pushed forth, up the hill.

Celtic and Iberian infantrymen charged down the hill, wielding immense three-foot blades. Their swords came down on the Romans' shields like ferocious hammers, but the Roman infantry swiftly cut them down. They formed the cohorts that Scipio had planned, confusing the enemy infantry's charge and increasing the distance between each enemy swordsman. Edetani soldiers were locked in combat with fellow Spanish tribesmen, clashing sword against sword. Laelius slashed and jabbed at every oncoming warrior. He was able to grab one Gallic swordsman by his bushy, bloody crimson beard and send him tumbling down the hill. He quietly thanked Scipio that he required his army to remain clean-shaven. Meanwhile, along the right side of the hill, Scipio's faction was gaining ground as well. His cohorts seemed to be working, isolating enemies from one another so that no soldier would be caught by a swordsman while trying to defend himself from another.

Numidian cavalrymen had begun to make their way down the incline as well. Expert horsemen, they were able to carefully descend toward the oncoming Roman army. However, Scipio's cavalry was well prepared to meet them. Hasdrubal Barca stood at the top of the hill, overseeing the battle. Beside him stood Massinissa, the commander of Hasdrubal's cavalry. Laelius watched Massinissa let loose a bone-shuddering cry and descend into the fray. Hasdrubal, however, remained where he was, sometimes directing another barrage of stones, but mostly observing and calculating.

Gradually, the tides began to turn. It was as if a great river had begun flowing in the opposite direction, and instead of Celtic, Numidian, and Carthaginian forces rushing down upon the Romans, Scipio's army steadily forced them up the hill backward. Scipio and Laelius spotted one another at the farthest ends of the battle. Scipio made a sign, which Laelius confirmed, and the two directed the Roman army to charge the camp. Though outnumbered by swordsmen and cavalry, each of Scipio's cohorts became fiercer. Once they had gained the upper hand, their advance upward was unstoppable.

As Scipio reached the edge of the enemy camp, he realized

that Hasdrubal Barca was no longer there and the camp had been deserted. A Numidian horseman rode up to Scipio, ready to take off the general's head, but Laelius speared the horseman's shoulder. Scipio swiftly cut him down and left his horse hysterical without a rider.

"Hasdrubal is gone," Scipio told Laelius. "Retreated."

Scipio searched the surrounding area, and then spotted the Carthaginian general leading what remained of his men off the hill. They had left Massinissa and the Numidian cavalry behind, though Scipio's army would grossly outnumber them.

"We've won, then?" Laelius confirmed, though he could see in Scipio's gaze following the escaping general that his friend would not consider this battle a resounding victory.

After the dust had settled, Massinissa had escaped as well, but the rest of the forces that had been left to fight the Romans had been captured as prisoners or lay slain on the hill. While Scipio was busy organizing the spoils of the Carthaginian camp, a triumvirate of Scipio's generals approached him.

"Hasdrubal is not far off," a veteran named Quintus informed Scipio. "If we send our men now, we may still be able to reach him."

Scipio thought on this for a moment, and Laelius, seeing his friend's hesitation, said, "If we allow him to get away with his men, he will only build a greater army against us. We must finish him once and for all."

Scipio pondered the matter, then replied, "Let him go for now. We must be patient. Our men are tired and worn after two long days of training and a grueling, well-fought battle. We still have much to sort through in the camp."

"But commander—" another general began, but Scipio stopped him with a firm hand.

"Celebrate. Offer your men congratulations, not another bone to fetch."

The generals nodded and departed to congratulate their various garrisons, but Laelius was not satisfied.

"Why allow Hasdrubal to escape? Why not proclaim this battle a victory for Rome?"

"This is a victory," Scipio countered.

Looking into Scipio's eyes, Laelius was struck by a sudden rush of optimism. He felt the immense wing-beats of Nike just overhead. The sun was brighter than it had been before, and the wind tasted sweeter. On that hilltop, the two friends shared a moment of clairvoyance. They saw Fortuna's footsteps in the Sands of Time preceding them on a great beach in a far-off shore that neither had seen before.

"Tell the men to release the Spanish and Numidian prisoners," Scipio instructed Laelius. "Let them tell their people of Rome's victory."

Chapter Nine

THE RAIN IN SPAIN—207 B.C.

Most men dream their entire lives to be called a king. Scipio, however, was unlike most men. After the Battle at Baecula, Spanish hostages and soldiers once loyal to Carthage flocked back to their tribes and villages. They told their wives, sons, neighbors, and chieftains of the man who had defeated the Carthaginian general who had terrorized their country for years. Many of the fighters were enthusiastic to join Scipio's army. All sang praises of Scipio's tactical brilliance. Due to the prominence and vast knowledge of Scipio's patrilineage, it was decided that he could not be a demigod—and besides, the Roman gods had not yet taken hold of the Spanish tribes. Thus, it was decided that Scipio must be a king, and the Spanish soldiers, chiefs, and kings throughout the Iberian Peninsula began to refer to him as such. While a majority of those in Scipio's position would accept the title as a compliment, Scipio took it as the gravest offense.

"Rome is a republic," Scipio vented to Laelius, "not a monarchy."

The two sat in Hasdrubal Barca's former tent. Through the open entryway, Laelius could see the great silver mines stretched forth in the distance. These had been Carthage's last claim on Iberia's public wealth.

"I have no right to be called a king, and yet every communication with our Spanish allies refers to me as such. Even the Roman infantry and cavalry have started bowing to me as king. It's ridiculous!"

"They wish to honor you," Laelius told his friend frankly.

"I don't deserve any more honor than the other men who fought valiantly. I'm no more kingly than they are. Is my entire army to be crowned and rule over our own kingdoms?"

"You've led these men to victory twice now. You've freed prisoners of Carthage and sent them back to their families. The people of Spain understand you as a glorious leader and champion. To them you have proven yourself as a king. The men you have led know your achievements firsthand and also believe you deserve a title greater than general—"

"In the Roman Republic, what could be greater than a great general?" Scipio asserted.

"They believe that you have proven yourself beyond that. You must understand this."

Scipio huffed and glared out past the mines. Laelius knew that his friend understood, but he also knew that Scipio's father's philosophy was deeply enmeshed in every fiber of Scipio's being. Every day, Laelius saw more of Publius the Elder in his son's face, reflecting his hold on Scipio's mind that had only solidified since Scipio's father's death. But Scipio was his own man who had achieved his own victories, and it was he, not his father, who would be proclaimed king. Laelius could sometimes see the trepidation in Scipio's eyes realizing that he was entering paths of glory on which his father had never tread. He saw such a look in his friend's eyes now. Laelius kept his speech soft and measured. Scipio was ever open to logic.

"If you are so offended by the title of king, then choose another—something beyond your military or political positions. Chief. Imperator. Something for those who wish to exalt you to place you above your peers," Laelius said.

"Fine. 'Imperator,' if 'general' or 'commander' will not satisfy them," Scipio grumbled.

Laelius nodded and left the tent immediately to disseminate the message.

As he departed, Scipio went back to studying one of his father's maps of southern Spain. They had received intelligence from an Edetani scout that, after weeks without word, Hasdrubal Barca had finally resurfaced and was recruiting more men. However, he was not the Roman army's only concern. Carthage had sent a new general, Hanno, across the Mediterranean. He and his army had landed at a southern port, miles from New Carthage, and met Mago. The Edetani scouts believed that Hasdrubal Barca joined Mago's army after retreating, hiding out in his comrade's army. The combined forces made them intimidating and difficult to approach the armies. Their movements were erratic throughout the country and, though the Edetani had said that Hasdrubal Barca was clearly recruiting more Spanish soldiers, the towns from which they came were spread throughout the south. The heart of the forces was indistinguishable from the skirmishers at the edge of the forces. Successfully isolating and attacking one of the general's armies would be near impossible without drawing the others into battle.

That evening, while Scipio and Laelius continued to study Publius the Elder's maps of the woods that the Carthaginian generals now occupied, General Silanus arrived with further intelligence. Silanus, whose right leg had been injured by a Carthaginian lance during a skirmish in Naples, walked with a slight limp that he had honed into a dignified swagger. He entered the commander's tent and propped himself against a chair.

"More intel from our Spanish allies," Silanus announced, "this time from Edeco's men near New Carthage."

"Hasdrubal Barca has extended past New Carthage?" Laelius asked, shocked.

"Not Hasdrubal Barca," Silanus corrected. "Hasdrubal Gisgo. With New Carthage in Roman hands, Hasdrubal Gisgo set up a new base for the Carthaginian armies at Gades."

"Any word on the whereabouts of Hasdrubal Barca and the other generals?" Scipio inquired.

"I assume they will eventually join Hasdrubal Gisgo at Gades, though there is no indication of such a meeting in their movements," Silanus said. "I propose sending a reconnaissance mission to pursue the Carthaginians' army and pinpoint their location."

"Any mission we send would run the risk of being detected and sparking a battle," Laelius reminded him. "If we send men to start following Carthaginian soldiers, we will have no idea if we are being led to Hasdrubal Barca and Mago or if we're being ambushed."

"Are you confident that you will be able to pursue the Carthaginians without detection?" Scipio asked Silanus.

Silanus nodded solemnly and adjusted his grip on the back of the chair.

"Take the men on the mission, then," Scipio instructed.

∽

A few weeks later, Silanus returned. Scipio had been mostly concerned with organizing the resources that had been won from Hasdrubal after the Battle at Baecula, most notably the silver mines. Oversight of the silver mines had been temporarily delegated to a garrison of Scipio's army, although Scipio had sent a barrage of messages to Rome to send a separate group to tend to the mines. He was busy training the army for the coming battle with the Carthaginian generals and had become irritated that one of his garrisons was falling behind in their training. He largely received silence from Rome after initial congratulations that he had taken the mines from Carthaginian hands. The unofficial word was that, as usual, Rome was more concerned by the military actions in Italy than those farther afield. Evidently, most of their gaze was directed toward General Nero's legion in northern Italy. Scipio was discussing with Laelius his intention of sending another message to the city when Silanus entered the tent.

"Silanus!" Scipio exclaimed, understandably shocked to see the man he had sent out months ago. "What's the matter?"

Silanus chuckled sheepishly. "I am surprised none of my men preceded me with the news."

"What news?" Scipio insisted. "Have we located the generals?"

"Located them?" Silanus laughed. "We've exploded their alliance! During the reconnaissance mission, a battle did indeed spring up between our garrison and the Carthaginians, but Fortuna smiled on Rome again! It was a spectacular battle, but the spoils are even greater! Hanno has been captured, Mago has fled to join Hasdrubal Gisgo at the base in Gades, and Hasdrubal Barca is retreating to Gaul to rendezvous with his brother."

"Hannibal?" Scipio muttered, unable to absorb all this glorious news at once.

He ran to the chest in which he kept his father's maps. Swiftly but gingerly, he extracted a map of the northern Italian border, laid it out, and studied it.

"Hasdrubal Barca will run directly into Nero's forces in Italy. Silanus, ride to General Nero as fast as you can and tell him to expect Hasdrubal Barca," Scipio commanded.

Silanus nodded and saluted.

"The rest of us will prepare to meet Mago and Hasdrubal Gisgo on the battlefield," Scipio told Laelius, who could see the ideas in his mind beginning to spark.

"Oh, and Commander," Silanus said, gripping the edge of the tent's opening as he exited, "I brought a guest who wishes to speak with you."

Scipio looked to Laelius, perplexed. "Let him enter."

Silanus left, and in his place stood a hooded figure. His cloak was made of a fabric that Laelius did not recognize; it was exotic and regal, but well worn with travel. The figure stood not much taller than Scipio, but more slender. His hands were dark. He walked slightly off-kilter, as if he were more comfortable riding horseback or, as Laelius suspected, accustomed to wearing a sword that weighed down one side of his body. He had likely given it to one of Silanus's soldiers before entering the tent. He was a friend here. The figure lifted the cloak from his face. Massinissa, the commander of Hasdrubal Barca's cavalry, stood before them.

"Great Imperator," Massinissa addressed Scipio.

Laelius saw his friend tense at the title. He still was not entirely happy with his concession.

Massinissa continued, "I wish to extend my most humble thanks for the return of my nephew. After the battle on this very hill was ended, I feared the worst for my cavalry, and especially my sister's eldest son. He is a good boy and a great rider. So you can imagine how overjoyed I was when he arrived at our camp unharmed, speaking to your justness and valiance. Flattery and gratitude, however," Massinissa went on, his brow darkening, "are not the only reasons for my visit. I come to you in the utmost secrecy because I believe that you and I can help one another."

Scipio nodded and sat, gesturing for Massinissa to do so as well. The Numidian commander complied and continued.

"My father was the king of what was once the most powerful nation in Numidia. I, as his first-born son, am destined to take his throne. I have recently learned of my father's passing, but what is worse, in my absence, a pretender has taken my throne. And a man named Syphax, who rules over another Numidian nation, is supporting the pretender's claim in an effort to increase his own influence in Numidia. I have the sovereign right to rule over my father's kingdom, but I cannot defeat Syphax's forces alone. He controls one of the most powerful armies in the region, second only to Carthage. However, if Rome supports my claim to the throne, I may well be able to regain what is rightfully mine."

"And what do you offer in return?" Scipio asked.

"My men and I will leave the Carthaginian army immediately. Without us, their cavalry will be more than halved. We will return to our home across the sea and win back our country. We can be a powerful ally to Rome in Africa."

"Why do you imagine Rome would need allies in Africa?" Scipio countered.

Massinissa smirked in response. "As I told you, I come to you in secrecy. There are many people—Hannibal, Hasdrubal Gisgo, Syphax—who would love to hang me as a traitor for orchestrating this meeting and claim my men as their own. I might be dead by tomorrow morning if you exposed me. But I believe that you are a shrewd leader. You know that I am more valuable as a living ally than a dead enemy." Massinissa stood. "I will not be far off tonight, but I must return to my men in the morning before my absence is detected. Inform me of your decision when you come to it." He replaced his hood and took his leave.

Scipio sat for a great many minutes, staring down at the grass a few feet off, thinking to himself. Laelius noticed his lips move pensively, but no sound emerged from them.

After what seemed like an eternity of contemplation, Laelius said, "He is right. Allies in Africa would give Rome an enormous advantage against Carthage. Imagine Rome's possibilities with an allied nation right at Carthage's doorstep. Besides, it would limit a major source of Carthage's cavalry—and without Massinissa's Numidian riders, our legion might actually stand a chance against the armies at Gades."

"I know," Scipio finally said, quiet as a grave, "but Laelius, he killed my father and my uncle. Without him, they might still be alive. I cannot be his ally."

Laelius was silent. Now it was his turn to contemplate. Finally, he asked, "Do you remember that first winter you invited me to your home?"

"Of course."

"Do you remember a conversation you had with your father? Over dinner? About what it would take to win the war once and for all?"

Scipio nodded. He had evidently had that conversation on his mind as well.

"Do you believe that you can be that general? Do you believe that you can be the one to lead us across the Mediterranean and end this war?"

"I do not know," Scipio murmured, "but I believe in Rome. I believe in her people. I believe that Rome can win this war."

"Rome has chosen you," Laelius said.

Scipio was struck by this. Even after all he had accomplished, he obviously did not consider himself worthy of such recognition. Laelius was amazed at his friend's humility after all this time.

"I believe this is that moment in which you must choose to take up the sword that Rome wishes you to take," Laelius said gently. "Without Massinissa, without an ally in Africa, there will be no end to this war, certainly not on Carthage's shores."

Scipio did not speak for a great while. The crickets began to chirp in the fields, signaling the end of dusk. The silver stillness just before the sun dipped below the horizon was passing. Nighttime was not a safe time for indecision. It was a time for action. The moon commanded the waves, the nocturnal creatures awoke, and those who slumbered lived fantastic lives in their dreams. The dark was not a precipice; it was an ultimatum. All choices, after all, were made in the dark. No man truly knows the choices he is making until their repercussions are long past the point of no return. So Laelius watched his friend, who had won and lost so much in the years they had known one another, decide in the dark, lit only by the growling, amber light from the brazier. Finally, Laelius saw that he had made his choice.

"For Rome?" Laelius ventured.

"For Rome," Scipio nodded.

The following morning, Scipio met with Massinissa and agreed to his terms. Rome would support Massinissa's claim to his father's throne and would in turn gain a powerful ally across the Mediterranean. Massinissa returned to his men and, much to the dismay of the Carthaginians, immediately transported them back to Africa to fight Syphax's forces.

After Scipio received word that Nero had intercepted and defeated Hasdrubal Barca, he saw that the end of Carthage's occupation of Spain was near. He put his brother, Lucius, in charge of attacking Spanish towns still loyal to the Carthaginians, knowing that it would draw Mago and Hasdrubal Gisgo out from their safe haven in Gades. In the meantime, he honed his men into more fierce and strategic warriors than they had ever been. Though the new, combined Carthaginian forces vastly outnumbered Scipio's army, Scipio was confident in his men, in their training, and in their passion. Laelius found him in the mornings looking out from the hilltop toward Gades, challenging Mago and Hasdrubal Gisgo, waiting to catch a glimpse of his armies marching toward Baecula.

His wish finally came true after Lucius attacked Orongis, a small village of Carthaginian sympathizers. Only a few miles away from New Carthage, Orongis had been one of the first towns to be won over by the Carthaginians when they landed in Spain, and it proved to be the last straw. One afternoon, a scout returned to the Roman camp with news that Hasdrubal Gisgo and Mago were marching to Ilipa, just a stone's throw from Scipio's camp at Baecula. The next day, Scipio organized his men and marched to confront the combined Carthaginian armies. They approached the valley cautiously, planning to set up camp on the near side with an open view of the thousands of Carthaginian infantry, cavalry, and war elephants atop Ilipa's low hills.

"Send a garrison of the cavalry beneath that ledge," Scipio

instructed Laelius. "If Mago tries to attack while we build the camp, they can defend the rest of the army."

Laelius agreed and a band of Carthaginian cavalry descended on them from the enemy camp. Laelius and his men did away with them swiftly. He guessed that Mago had sent them as scouts to gauge Scipio's tactical intuition. His answer lay with the few riders retreating up the hill. When he returned to tell Scipio of the skirmish, he found the commander meeting with Silanus.

"This is totally unnecessary," the general harrumphed, supporting himself on the end of a chair. "I am much more help to you here at the camp with the rest of the army."

"It is not your place to decide what is necessary and where you will be of the most help to this army," Scipio challenged. "You will accompany Edeco's men and retrieve the infantry and horses that Chief Culchas promised because I have commanded you to do so. Go now; you'll gain more ground before nightfall."

Silanus left the tent in evident disgruntlement.

"You're sending Silanus to retrieve some men and horses from a Spanish chief?" Laelius asked.

Scipio grunted in the affirmative.

"Isn't that a simple errand?" Laelius inquired. "Shouldn't Edeco's men be able to deliver them without a general?"

"Regardless, Silanus will be with them," Scipio said. He seemed troubled, and all at once Laelius understood.

"You don't trust the Spanish."

Scipio said nothing.

Laelius continued, "They're your allies, but you don't trust them."

"No," Scipio finally admitted. "I will not repeat my father's mistake. I *accept* allies. I do not trust them."

Laelius nodded, but the finality of his friend's statement lit the tiniest fire in him—a question that burned in the back of his mind, one he dared not ask for the gravity of its answer.

Heavy clouds loomed overhead on the morning of the battle. The sky hung gray over the dark ridges of the valley. Scipio's men faced the Carthaginian camp. Scipio had instructed that they all wake up early, eat breakfast, and prepare for battle. On Scipio's command, the first garrisons ascended the hill to attack the camp. The first infantrymen reached the camp just as the sun was peaking like a sickly silver orb above the hills. The response was swift: Hasdrubal and Mago whipped their men into battle formation, exactly as Scipio had planned. Now, the Romans waited.

As the Carthaginians started to descend the hill, the sky opened up and a torrential downpour rained on the Spanish valley. The grass became soft and the rocks slick, causing the descending Carthaginian infantry to slip and tumble down. Scipio and his generals sprang into action. With Scipio leading the right wing and Silanus and Laelius on the left, the remaining Roman army enveloped the descending Carthaginians. Scipio had trained the cavalry to leap from their horses, gripping their manes in one hand while slicing their enemies with their powerful swords in the other. Some of the infantry took to spooking the war elephants, sending them stampeding into the Carthaginian infantry or trampling the camp. The storm roared as the battle raged on, the grass soaked with mud and blood. Soon, the Carthaginian forces were in place. As the strong, wet winds whipped Scipio's cheek, he gave the final signal, and the army closed in on the enemy.

Hours later, the storm subsided, and the sun emerged with all its golden brilliance. The grass glowed like the morning sea, speckled with shiny pearls of raindrops. Murdered men lay sprawled over the hillside. Scipio gazed out over the carnage, and then beyond, past the edge of the valley and the shimmering hills. He looked over a land that was now free from tyranny. Rome was victorious. Carthage's hold on Spain had finally been thwarted.

Chapter Ten

DINNER IN SIGO—206 B.C.

O nce the Carthaginian forces had been ousted from Spain, Scipio immediately set his sights across the sea. The sudden and enormous victories on the Iberian Peninsula sent the Roman Senate reeling and scrambling to organize the newly acquired land and resources. While the senate adjusted to Europe's new layout, Scipio had time to plan. On a warm summer evening, Scipio invited Laelius into the commander's tent to discuss their next move.

"The city of Carthage," Scipio reminded his friend, "lies at the northeastern edge of the African coast, just a few days southwest of Sicily. The senate in Carthage controls the city and the military, which in turn exercises their control over the kingdoms of Numidia to the west. By marching west, crossing into Iberia and conquering the Alps, Hannibal infiltrated Rome's home country. When the First War beat Carthage back from Sicily, Hannibal found another way."

Scipio heaved a thoughtful sigh. "We have been celebrating

our victory against Mago and Hasdrubal Gisgo for weeks now, but all I have been able to think of are my father's words long ago—the words you reminded me about. Carthage will always find another way. To end this war is to defeat Carthage itself. As long as the city stands, they will find another way to get at Rome."

A warm breeze rustled the tent and displaced a few of his curls. "Massinissa now marches as an ally to Rome," Scipio continued. "Should he regain his father's throne, he will be a powerful asset in a Roman campaign across the sea, but it will not be enough. We will have to surround Carthage completely, drawing all of its neighbors to march with Rome."

"So, what do you suggest?" Laelius inquired.

"Syphax, the man supporting Massinissa's usurper, is the most powerful Numidian king. With both him and Massinissa as Rome's allies, the other, smaller principalities will fall in with them."

Laelius hummed reservedly, considering Scipio's plan. He had heard stories of Syphax from some of the Iberian riders who had fought alongside Massinissa's cavalry in the Carthaginian army. He was rumored to be clever and cunning, a shrewd negotiator with opulent habits. Syphax was also hungry for power. He had gained most of his military and his kingdom through strategic attacks and political maneuvering with little remorse for those who stood in his way. His domain had grown so large that it had two capitals, though Syphax was primarily stationed in his palace in the western capital of Sigo. He was said to host extravagant feasts, inviting neighboring princes and generals to dine with him in his glorious abode. However, few of his guests left without paying some sort of price: Sometimes it was a payment to Syphax's treasury or a transference of land or resources; other times it was their life.

One story that had struck Laelius was the disappearance of a young Numidian prince who had visited one of Syphax's feasts. The prince was the only heir of a friendly neighboring kingdom famous for their iron mines. He was immature and foolish, and, upon arriving, reveled in the opulence that was presented to him in Syphax's palace. The prince was bombarded with delicious food, potent drink, beautiful women, and the finest accommodations. There seemed to be no end to the pleasure until, one day, it all stopped. The people of the city no longer saw the prince lounging about the palace grounds, bladder of wine in hand. Syphax's slaves ceased buying fine silks and colorful fruits and sweets in large numbers. The music and raucous celebrations that once penetrated late into the evening slipped into silence overnight. The prince never returned home.

The Iberian cavalryman who had told Laelius this tale admitted that it might all be speculation and rumor. But what was curious and undeniably true was that a few weeks later, Syphax sent a garrison to the prince's aging father, supposedly to pay their respects as others had. Even more curious was that a few months later when the aged king died, he had left his land, his people, and all the iron mines to Syphax. Whatever the king had learned from the garrison must have convinced him to turn his kingdom over to Syphax. Yes, Syphax would be a powerful ally to Rome, but at what cost?

Scipio was no fool, Laelius thought, and would have also heard these stories. "What is your plan for Syphax, then? It will be too dangerous to send you and, even if Syphax can be trusted, your absence here would leave the army vulnerable."

"You're right," Scipio agreed, "which is why I would like to send you on my behalf while I remain with the army. There is no man I trust more than you, Laelius. I know you understand the kind of ruler he is, and you will resist whatever temptations he may place before you."

Laelius nodded, and the two agreed that he would march to the coast with a small garrison in the morning to sail to Sigo.

The coast at the western edge of Syphax's kingdom was pleasantly cool. Whereas the city farther inland was overcome with oppressive humidity, the free sea air whisked the heat off into the heavens. Laelius waited in the small tent that the garrison had built, sitting directly on the hard stones. He was still recovering from his journey across the Mediterranean and the sensation of the solid ground comforted his tumultuous stomach. He had sent a messenger disguised in Numidian military garb to request an audience with Syphax when they first landed. That was two days ago. Since then Laelius had simply waited. Sometimes he would look off toward the sea, but this usually made him queasy. He spent most hours staring out upon the great continent of Africa—beautiful, golden, and novel. Few Romans had set foot on its shores, let alone explored the countries deep within. Laelius always felt a rush of pride when he realized how unique his position was.

Finally, a soldier entered Laelius's tent and informed him that Syphax was approaching with a small court. Laelius exited the tent and gathered his garrison to greet the approaching dignitaries.

Syphax wore a deep red tunic of the finest fabric that spilled over his shoulders and pooled in the small wells of sand at his feet. He had a shock of black curls that tumbled from the crown of his head over his ears and across his forehead, interrupted by a golden band that circled his head. His face was hard, as if an expert sculptor's masterpiece had come to life, but his amber, almond-shaped eyes were bright and his lips bore a lively smirk. He was being shaded by two nearly nude slaves, each holding a palm decorated with ostrich features.

"General Laelius," Syphax sang jovially as if the two were old friends reunited, "the favorite of General Scipio. I have been paying very close attention to the war across the sea, and I must say that Rome has kept me on the edge of my seat! One battle after another, you seem to be beating the Carthaginians back again and again! We really find it thrilling, don't we?" His court chuckled mechanically. "And you have to believe me, I have been rooting for the Romans this entire time. I always root for the winning team." Syphax winked coyly at Laelius. "But I have to admit that I did not foresee that fantastic performance at Ilipa. What a show! And now, the whole of Iberia in Roman hands? I can only imagine what the seats in Europe must be like." He sighed wistfully and stared through Laelius and past the crashing waves.

"Then it seems," Laelius ventured, "that we are already on the same side."

Syphax's eyes flashed back to Laelius. He smiled. He had rehearsed this meeting many times, Laelius realized. Only now, it was showtime.

"Of course," Syphax said coolly. "As I said, I always side with the winners."

"Then you are open to the treaty that was mentioned in the message—"

"Yes, I was intrigued by your message," Syphax interrupted.

"A disguised messenger at my palace door, a secret meeting at the coast with a Roman general—very exciting! But unfortunately, this really isn't my style. I'll tell you what. Why don't you and Scipio come to dine at my palace in Sigo. You will be welcomed as guests and treated to the greatest pleasures that this country has to offer."

"That isn't possible," Laelius insisted. "We are in a foreign country, influenced by the Carthaginians. Surely you can understand the need for discretion. Besides, Scipio is needed in Spain to lead the army. He sends me as his right hand and ear, ready to discuss and carry out whatever terms the two of us agree on."

Syphax offered a saccharine smile and gestured to the two slaves shading him. "These are my favorite slaves. I simply don't know what I would do without them. I place in them my utmost trust and compassion. Now, if I sent either of my slaves over the sea to request an audience with your General Scipio, do you think he would accept?"

Laelius tried to remain expressionless, but some small movement must have confirmed Syphax's point.

"I, too, have standards, and when I make a deal with a man, I make it with *him*, not his favorite," Syphax continued. "A hand and an ear are flattering, General, but I'm afraid I cannot ratify a formal treaty without the full package. It is, as you said, not possible."

With that, Syphax turned and took his leave with the rest of his court.

Scipio paced in a slow circle inside the commander's tent. "We need Syphax's allegiance if we are ever to achieve victory in a siege of Carthage."

"It is too dangerous," Laelius insisted. "Despite what he says, Syphax has been allied with the Carthaginians up until this point."

"But we're gaining ground against them," Scipio said. "Syphax is self-serving. If he actually believes that Rome has become superior to Carthage, I can convince him to ally with us."

"Or perhaps Syphax has realized that you are the key to a Roman victory and is planning to turn you over to the Carthaginians."

"I have to go, Laelius. Syphax has challenged me, and I cannot back down—not without sacrificing my honor and my pride."

"Well, if you're insisting," Laelius said, "then I'm going with you."

Scipio and Laelius set sail for the capital city of Sigo with the smallest garrison manageable, hoping to draw as little attention to themselves as possible. They left the army in the dead of night. Scipio gave his generals command of the army and instructed them to relocate back to Tarraco. Only his brother, Lucius Scipio, knew where the two men were headed, in case anything should happen to both of them. Wrapped in dark cloaks that shielded them from the cold sea winds and disguised their military uniforms, the two friends made their way across the water.

As Laelius had just made the same journey, he watched his friend take in the new landscape. It felt humbling to be in the center of the Mediterranean sailing far from one's home to a strange, new land. The world seemed so small and yet so vast from their modest boat. But Scipio, as always, was only emboldened by the adventure. When the captain of the boat spotted land, Scipio stood taller. His gaze was sharp. To Scipio, Africa was a land of endless possibilities.

As they approached the port of Sigo, Scipio and Laelius both immediately caught sight of a small fleet of Carthaginian ships. Laelius told the captain to sail cautiously, as out of sight of the ships as possible. Though the port itself did not offer many places to hide, the captain was clever and wove behind the many merchant ships coming and going through the port. He would give Scipio and Laelius just enough time to peek at the fleet before darting behind another merchant vessel. That is how Scipio was able to catch a glimpse of Hasdrubal Gisgo disembarking from one of the ships.

"By Jupiter, Syphax is going to hand you over to Carthage!" Laelius exclaimed. "We have to turn back; it is too dangerous."

"Syphax is clever," Scipio countered. "If he were going to turn me over to Hasdrubal Gisgo, he would not let them moor their ships in plain sight. Whatever his plan is, I think it's safe to assume that he won't give us over to Carthage—at least, not yet."

"We'll have to be cautious. Even if it isn't Syphax's plan to make you a Carthaginian prisoner, that doesn't mean Hasdrubal Gisgo's men won't try, given the chance."

Scipio agreed and the two disembarked with the rest of Scipio's garrison onto a small, deserted platform.

Syphax's capital city reflected the Numidian king's own adoration of the eclectic and exotic. Ships sailed into its port from Italy, Carthage, Numidia, Greece, Iberia, and a great many other principalities across Africa and the Mediterranean bearing fabrics, jewels, weaponry, spices, livestock, slaves, and anything else that might be traded at the Sigo marketplace. Thieves and young stowaways often sneaked into the city on these ships as well, hoping to find more fruitful work in Sigo. From early morning late evening, the city was a bustling cacophony of different people.

The smells of exotic foods being prepared touched Laelius's nose. Every few steps that they took, he heard yet another language spoken in hurried, often confrontational tones. Beggars sat on the street asking for food or a moment of kindness. Small children ran about the market, picking unsuspecting pockets. Women dressed in beautiful skirts and bodices made of the finest silk danced with fans or scarves. Goats bleated, pigs snorted, monkeys chittered, and parrots recited poetry for coins. Concealed in their swiftly overheating cloaks, Scipio and Laelius maneuvered their way through the menagerie of the marketplace. Laelius's eyes darted between every shadow that might conceal danger. Sigo catered to as many kidnappers, murderers, and spies as it did merchants and diplomats.

"The palace is up this next street," Scipio muttered to Laelius. "Stay vigilant."

Turning up the narrow street, the grounds of the enormous palace came into view. The walls were in some places golden; in other places bleached pearl white by the sun. Gigantic flowering vines dripped from the lower windows into green gardens, with paths and pools that wound around the outside of the audacious structure in the center. White peacocks wandered about the grounds, every now and then pecking at a pink or orange blossom. Two ferocious stone lions guarded the door, crouched and ready to pounce on any intruder with ill will. Scipio and his garrison passed these two guardians and ascended the steps to find a massive relief of a lion's face above the door, as if forever roaring into the city streets. The garrison removed their cloaks, revealing their identity, and Syphax's guard allowed them into the palace.

Syphax greeted his guests accompanied by his two favorite slaves, this time holding two gargantuan fans rimmed with peacock feathers. Behind him stood two female slaves carrying bowls of grapes and other ripe fruit. This time his tunic was a more purple shade of red, the color of freshly spilled blood. He had the same instantly familiar demeanor with Scipio that he had shown to Laelius.

"Welcome!" Syphax laughed, approaching the group. "I am so honored to be in the presence of the great commander at last." He offered an extravagant bow, causing Scipio to blush, though only Laelius noticed.

"We are honored to be your guests," Scipio said.

"During your stay, you will only receive the best that Sigo has to offer. If there is anything that is not to your liking, please let me know and I will ameliorate it. If there are any pleasantries that you desire beyond those you see before you, rest assured that they will be brought to you."

Syphax snapped his fingers and the two slaves with fruit bowls approached. They offered the fruit to Laelius and Scipio, posing at a provocative angle. Scipio and Laelius both politely partook of the fruit.

"Incidentally," Syphax went on, "we will be joined by a surprise guest this evening. I'm sure you are acquainted—"

"In fact, we saw him disembarking at the port," Scipio said.

Syphax's flashy smile fell a bit hearing that his surprise had been spoiled, but in seconds he perked back up again.

"Well, I look forward to having two of the greatest generals of the war seated at my table." He bowed again and departed.

The women passed off the fruit bowls to another slave and showed Scipio and Laelius to their rooms. Their accommodations were pleasantly adjacent, each with a canopied bed fitted with Egyptian cotton sheets, gold-lined furniture, and a gorgeous view of the gardens. The women asked if they could provide

Scipio and Laelius with any other services, which they declined. The women were relieved and graciously took their leave.

"Nothing short of spectacular, I suppose," Scipio mused.

"Syphax is all spectacle," Laelius moaned. "He treats war as if it is some sort of amusing game or performance."

"Yes," Scipio said, "but it's easy enough to play a part."

Laelius decided to explore the palace a bit more and told Scipio he would meet him again before dinner. Curious to see what wonders he might behold, Laelius strolled through the wide white halls decorated with fantastic murals of lion hunts, chariot races, gladiators triumphing, and epic battles. He had never seen anything so ostentatious. But his wandering stopped abruptly when he heard a familiar voice just around the corner.

"Carthage has done well by you, and will again," Hasdrubal Gisgo asserted gruffly.

Laelius pressed himself against the wall to keep from being seen as he listened.

"The Carthaginians have been defeated yet again," Syphax chuckled, "and you know I hate losing."

"It was a minor setback—"

"Minor? Ha! My friend, you had a firm grip on the Iberian Peninsula and it was torn away from you. You lost your hold on Europe. Carthage has barely any more men in Europe than in their city in the east. You have made no permanent gains since the First War was started. What sort of an investment would I be making?"

"Hannibal is still in Italy," Hasdrubal Gisgo reminded Syphax, "and Carthage still has the power to take your city from you if we wish. Do you think you will still be choosing between which side may win or lose when you have nothing?"

"Yes . . . well," Syphax grumbled, "Hannibal is certainly a

significant factor in all of this, and I have not forgotten our history. We are, after all, neighbors. But it is as I said, my friend: I hate losing."

After Laelius informed Scipio that Hasdrubal Gisgo had come to convince Syphax to maintain his allegiance to Carthage, Scipio became a man on a mission.

At dinner, the table was laid with a banquet of rice, breads, fruit, cured meats, wild boar, olive oil, eel, fish, and colorful vegetables. Slaves milled about with golden platters, serving the guests the different courses that lay before them. Scipio and Laelius sat beside one another on a blood-red chaise—the same color as Syphax's tunic—across from Hasdrubal Gisgo and his men. Syphax sat at the head of the table, and while one of his favorite slaves fanned him, the other dropped grapes into his mouth when he snapped his fingers. He sat on an extravagantly decorated couch of the most outrageous purple with gold trim.

However, all eyes were on Scipio. Throughout the entire evening, Scipio spoke with such grace and charm that it was difficult not to become entranced by him. Even when Syphax attempted to derail the conversation by bringing up subjects such as Ilipa, the Battle at Baecula, Hannibal's proximity to Rome, and even the fatal betrayal of Scipio's father, Scipio politely and coolly evaded them and continued onto a more amicable topic.

Toward the end of the meal, as they ate a delicious concoction of figs and other fruit with which Laelius was not familiar, Scipio made a toast to their hospitable and glorious host. Surprisingly, Hasdrubal Gisgo then stood and offered a toast.

"I have spoken with many Romans and many Roman generals," he said. "But now I see why the Roman people offer you such a special place in their hearts. Never before have I met a man with as much gravitas as you, General Scipio. You are a great general, but I am pleased to know now that you are also a great man."

As Hasdrubal Gisgo lifted his glass, both sides of the dining room erupted in applause.

As Scipio's garrison prepared to set sail and meet the rest of the army at Tarraco, Syphax approached Scipio.

"You are a singular man, General Scipio," Syphax hummed. This time his two favorite slaves simply stood behind him, gazing stoically at nothing in particular. "Only a singular man would attempt to lay siege to the city of Carthage." He smirked. "That is your plan, isn't it? Why you need my support?"

"Yes," Scipio said frankly. "It is."

"Do you believe that you can do it?"

"Without you, we won't have a chance. But with you," Scipio smiled, "we will not lose."

"Well, then . . . leave some of your men here to oversee the ratification of the treaty of allegiance that your favorite, Laelius, proposed initially. I presume the terms have not changed?"

Scipio agreed and Syphax departed, followed by his slaves.

"I still don't trust him," Laelius cautioned.

"Alliances aren't about trust," Scipio said. "They're about playing the part."

Chapter Eleven

SCIPIO THE SOLDIER—206 B.C.

That summer, Scipio fell gravely ill. Though he had been prone to bouts of sickness in his youth, they were nothing compared to this. The illness was mysterious and vicious. Some medics guessed it might be a corruption of the blood, but they said so with reservations. Scipio was bedridden for months, on the edge of consciousness. Most nights, Laelius sat by his bedside or outside of his tent. He began to lose so much sleep that he, too, looked sickly. Lucius and some of the other generals insisted that Laelius rest, as he was no good to them bedridden as well. Summer ticked slowly by, each day bleeding into another. Through the fog of his despair, Laelius sometimes could not discern whether the sun was rising or setting. The sun's warmth and the joyous twittering of young birds felt like a mockery. Laelius descended into a depression almost as potent as his friend's illness.

Then rumors began to circulate that Scipio had, in fact, died. When Laelius first heard this from a soldier, he ran as fast as his legs could carry him to the other end of the camp. He burst into Scipio's tent, only to discover him tossing in the clutches of a fever dream. Laelius calmed his friend, and as soon as Scipio descended into a peaceful slumber, Laelius marched back to the soldier with a fire in his eyes. But then he heard the whole story: that Scipio had died months ago, just after returning from Africa, and the other generals were keeping his death a secret to confuse the Carthaginians. Laelius vehemently asserted that Scipio was ill but living, though he sensed the soldier's skepticism.

The worst news came on the hottest day of that summer. Sweat dripped down the back of Laelius's neck, his forehead, and forearms when Lucius approached him. Two of their Spanish allies had begun a revolt against the Roman military. The brothers Indibilis and Mandonius had heard that Scipio had died and that the Roman army was undergoing a transition of leadership. Knowing that the army would be weak, they raised an army of their own people. The princes compared Roman rule to the Carthaginian occupation, preaching that the Spanish tribes alone should rule Spain. Their army had begun devastating towns north of the Ebro that were allied with Rome. Neither Lucius nor Laelius knew how to react against the princes' revolt.

Over the coming weeks, the bad news became worse. As Indibilis and Mandonius's men tore through the countryside attacking towns and Roman outposts, the soldiers in Scipio's army became restless. Talk of mutiny began spreading like a virus, infecting Roman troops throughout the Spanish countryside. The other generals optimistically denounced the talk as without substance: It was the heat, or it had been too long since the men had experienced a good fight, or it might have been their way of mourning their sick commander. The generals shut down such talk when they could and paid it little credence.

A few weeks after Laelius received word on Indibilis and Mandonius's mutiny, another soldier arrived announcing that the soldiers stationed at the Sucro River had rebelled in protest. They were being denied their pay in arrears and therefore renounced their allegiance to Rome. Once again, the generals were at a loss without their commander. They considered sending a legion to squelch the protest, but they worried those men might very well join the rebellion. Morale among all the Roman soldiers, even those still loyal, was at a record low. The army was in shambles, chaotic and demoralized. Laelius saw only one solution: They desperately needed Scipio back.

The day that Scipio's fever broke, Laelius remained by his side from morning until night. He fed him, bathed him, and offered him as much news and counsel as he believed his friend could take in his current state. A week later, under Laelius's devoted care, Scipio had physically recovered completely. His ego, however, had taken a dramatic blow.

"Mutiny," he muttered, eating bread and warm porridge with Laelius beside him. "I never would have thought . . . . Indibilis and Mandonius do not surprise me. They were fair-weather allies from the start. But Roman soldiers, true Roman men, rebelling?"

Scipio sighed and sullenly dropped his spoon into the porridge. Laelius watched it slowly sink into the gooey mush.

"I grew up among soldiers," Scipio said, dejected. "I thought I knew them through and through, but if they don't believe that they are being treated fairly, if they would rather fight on their own . . . ." He looked down at his feet. "I must have made a grave mistake. I am not the leader they thought I was."

"That's ridiculous," Laelius snapped. "You are the greatest

commander these men have ever known. You have led them to victory many times. But men have short and convenient memories." He grabbed Scipio's hand and earnestly looked him in the eye. "You have to remind them who you are."

This gave Scipio more confidence, and he rose from his seat to begin pacing. "Very well. Before we pursue Indibilis and Mandonius, we must face our own disillusioned countrymen. Send word for the legion at the Sucro River to meet with me at New Carthage, either as individuals or as a whole. There, we may discuss the matter of their payment face-to-face."

The rebels from the Sucro River accepted Scipio's invitation. Laelius and Scipio awaited their arrival on the steps of the city. Scipio looked on bravely as the band of rebels approached, but Laelius kept his hand on the hilt of his sword. He was not sure of Scipio's plan. The penalty for mutiny was severe and the men's betrayal had hit a personal nerve in Scipio. These were ambitious men as well, and should they decide to take action against Scipio, Laelius would be ready.

The men were all hard-faced and emotionless. They were led by an old veteran, Marcus, who arrived at the bottom step directly opposite Scipio. Marcus stood defiantly, his chest puffed out and his back, legs, and arms in almost mockingly perfect military posture. He had a white scar over his left eye from a skirmish with the Carthaginian cavalry. The men behind him exuded a similar pride and brashness. Many had grown blooming beards in opposition to Scipio's infamous suggestion to his army. Scipio, however, chose to ignore the men's attitudes.

"Countrymen," Scipio began, "for we are all countrymen, I understand that you believe that I have wronged you. Perhaps I have, and rest assured that you will be paid in full the arrears that were promised you. But I must ask you, my countrymen, is this payment worth the betrayal of our beloved Republic? Not only have you renounced me, but you have also renounced Rome. Under her banner, we defeated three of Carthage's most powerful generals. It is she who controls the principalities north of the Mediterranean. It is for her that we have marched so far from home, from our wives and children and those closest to us. It is Mother Rome who feeds us, who gives us strength and glory. Alone, we are but men. What is a soldier without a country for whom he fights? For what cause does he draw his sword? If he dies in battle, who performs his burial rites? There is no victory without Rome.

"My countrymen," Scipio went on, his voice dropping low, prompting many of the men to lean forward, "set aside your egos and accept Rome as your mother country yet again. I promise you amnesty for your mutiny if you pledge your loyalty to her now. Let us fight for her, and together we will help her attain glory!"

Marcus raised his sword with a triumphant "Yea!" More members of the crowd raised their swords in solidarity after seeing their leader respond positively to Scipio's overtures of patriotism.

A movement in the crowd caught Laelius's eye. Some of the mutineers were swiftly weaving their way toward the front. Laelius instinctively drew his sword, but before he could react, he saw a flash of metal and heard Marcus cry out. The sword fell from the old man's hand as blood leaked from the fresh wound in his side. The man who had killed him retracted his dagger and the old man collapsed.

The man who killed Marcus then lunged for Scipio, but he

was ready. Blade met blade and the two were locked in battle. Laelius tried to knock the aggressor off Scipio, but was engaged by another conspirator. Laelius cut him down swiftly, but another replaced him. Laelius knocked his dagger from his hand and shoved him down the stairs. As he tumbled down the steps, Laelius turned to witness Scipio felling the man who had murdered Marcus. Within minutes, the rest of the conspirators had been captured and brought to the prison below the city.

That evening, Scipio stood beside the pyre that the men had built outside of the city. He stared beyond the Spanish hills at the setting sun. The ruby and amber light stretched across the plains, submerging the green foliage in sacred gold and touching the edge of the wood at the base of the pyre. Marcus lay atop the carefully cultivated tower of pale wood. The blood had been quickly and thoroughly cleaned from his clothing. He had been given a newly polished uniform with a freshly dyed red cape. Charon's obol had been placed between his lips to enable his passage to the underworld. His shield was placed over his chest.

Laelius took his place beside Scipio and the two observed the garrison from the Sucro River carry torches and light the pyre. The structure caught immediately and burst into a gargantuan flame that singed hairs on Laelius's face. Soon, all of Scipio's forces stood at attention facing the flame. The great commander stepped forward. His face appeared jaundiced in the firelight. A few men came forward, presenting a sacrificial sow to Ceres as an offering to the chthonic gods to show mercy on the veteran.

Scipio spoke, "Here was a man who laid down his life for his Republic. He fought valiantly and believed in the power of the people. He—"

Scipio broke for a second, considering his words. Laelius and the rest of Scipio's men listened with bated breath.

"He died with honor and is presented to the gods with honor," Scipio continued. "Though he may have deserted his post, he did so because he believed his duty was unjust. He would not have his men mistreated, and so he did everything in his power to help them. He died for them. So, in the eyes of the men he fought for and beside, we celebrate his death with glory: for him, for the gods, and for the Republic."

As Scipio's last words echoed over the crackling of the burning wood, a quiet hum began to emanate from the crowd: "For the Republic."

The salute spread throughout the crowd, growing louder and more urgent until the walls of the city shook with a booming declaration: "For the Republic!"

Laelius looked to Scipio, who just moments ago had betrayed sadness and disappointment on his face that was quickly melting into pride. Laelius decided to join in with the rest: "For the Republic!" He repeated the phrase again and again, until finally, Scipio raised his sword high above his head. He opened his lips and his voice rang across the evening-blue mountains. His voice was the voice of ten thousand Romans, the voice of a city crying out across the European continent. The voice proclaimed its strength and its ambition. The voice shook the walls of the conquered city, surfed the waves across the Mediterranean, and kicked up the sand on the shores of a far-off land. Though it could never be said for sure, there were people residing in both Carthage and Rome who would swear years later that they heard a great echo rumble through the city streets that evening: "For the Republic!"

Two weeks after the veteran had been honored and his ashes

sent back to his family in Rome, Scipio arrived at Indibilis and Mandonius's camp in a deep valley a few miles from the Ebro River. The men of the Sucro River were now some of Scipio's most loyal infantrymen. The night of the veteran's funeral had made them more dedicated to the preservation of Rome's glory. Though Scipio appreciated the reclamation of these troops, he was single-minded as they marched past the Ebro. The two Spanish princes would have to be defeated. His father and uncle had fallen at the hands of rebellious Spanish troops. Scipio would not repeat their mistake.

The Roman army wove through the cavernous valley until they caught sight of the Spanish camp. The rebels had stationed themselves in a secure position against the rocks. The brothers' banner flew high above the tents. As soon as the army arrived, Laelius noticed a garrison approaching, led by the brothers. Indibilis and Mandonius stopped a few yards from Scipio.

Mandonius wore a snide smirk. "It seems the Great Imperator has resurrected from the dead," he announced.

The rest of the garrison snickered.

"Indibilis, Mandonius," stated Scipio with absolutely no humor in his voice, "you are indebted to Rome. You cannot betray her. Come back into her fold."

"We are not Rome's children," Indibilis snapped back. "She did not bear us or our forefathers or our sons. We are the sons of a noble land, unchained by war and Roman ruin. Ours is the land of great plains and mountains, and the greatest ocean. We are not the children of dogs."

"The grandeur of Spain and her children will whip Rome's little wolf pups," Mandonius laughed. "We shall send you scurrying home with your tails between your legs."

"You think because you defeated a few generals in a foreign

land, you can outmatch Spain's own forces?" Indibilis mocked. "Perhaps return to that sick bed."

"While your men quiver like dogs in a thunderstorm," Mandonius spat. "We are the thunder."

"So, turn back now or prepare to be trampled into Spanish dust."

With that, the two brothers turned and rode back to the camp.

Scipio's forces were visibly shaken. They had approached the camp with so much anticipation and pride, only to be ridiculed by two confident princes.

Laelius looked over at Scipio to ask how to proceed, but Scipio left no time.

He whipped his steed around to face his men and announced, "If you meant the oath you gave outside the walls of New Carthage, we shall not lose. We shall taste victory today, for no army can defeat the full force of Rome and her children. If you believe in Rome, then swear it: For the Republic!"

"For the Republic!" the army roared, and the battle had begun.

Scipio's army rushed toward the camp and met the Spanish rebels right at the edge. The two armies collided in a clash of iron. Men shouted, horses whinnied and shrieked, swords clanged, projectiles thudded, hooves stamped, men fell to the ground, shields scraped, helmets echoed, bones cracked, and the mountains themselves rumbled with outrage. It was a fantastic battle from the start. It sounded like thunder.

But if Spain was the thunder, then Rome was the lightning. As quickly as the battle had begun, Rome had the upper hand. Laelius saw only flashes of his countrymen cutting down their enemies like reapers in a field of wheat. Whether on horseback or on foot, wielding sword or sling, Rome was speedier than the princes' forces and swiftly halved their numbers of viable fighters. It was not long before Indibilis and Mandonius themselves were captured. The soldiers who had apprehended them brought them before Scipio. They began to beg for forgiveness and mercy, but Scipio stopped them. The valley was silent. A harsh streak of silver sliced through Scipio's eyes as he looked down on the rebel leaders.

Laelius worried that his friend might lose his temper, that he might issue a penalty more severe than death. In his heart, he began to panic. Did his friend see some justice in torturing these two brothers? Would he treat them as if they had been the Spanish troops who had betrayed his family? He could not allow Scipio to lose himself in this moment, not with all his men watching, not after they had lost and gained back so much! Laelius's heart raced. What could he do?

But Scipio surprised him yet again. He simply told the brothers, "You have known me as an enemy and as a friend: You may choose whether you prefer to keep Rome as an ally or enraged in anger against you."

The brothers immediately and emphatically pledged their allegiance to Rome. It was the most sincere Laelius had ever seen Mandonius and the most humble he had ever seen Indibilis. The two brothers were released back to their men and Scipio led his army north of the Ebro once more.

The Roman base was renamed Italica in honor of Rome's ongoing allegiance with the Spanish chieftains. As the summer cooled to fall, Scipio grew more and more anxious. With his illness having subsided and the resulting rebellions quashed, the time had come to make significant moves toward crossing the Mediterranean. Little communication had come from Massinissa or Syphax since their last meetings, but nevertheless, Scipio believed it was time.

One evening, he invited Laelius into the commander's tent. Immediately, Laelius noticed that all his friend's effects had been packed up. He knew what was coming.

"In order to convince the senate to approve a campaign across the sea," Scipio explained, "I will have to reenter the political sphere back in Rome. I'll have to lobby day and night for an unheard-of military expedition." Scipio sat and sighed, frustrated. "It's a prospect I'm not too excited about."

"You've hated being a politician," Laelius agreed.

"Yes, and this will be the hardest campaign to convince the consuls of yet," Scipio muttered. He stared down at the floor.

Laelius hated seeing his friend so despondent. "But it is your duty. If you believe that it is what you must do for the Republic, then you will do it," Laelius insisted. "You are a soldier, after all."

Scipio nodded hesitantly.

The next morning, he and Laelius left the Roman forces in the hands of Silanus and Marcius, and the two friends set off for the city.

Chapter Twelve

FIRE AND SWORD—205 B.C.

During her husband's absence, Aemelia had only become more influential in Roman society. She was a paragon of Roman womanhood: glamorous and independent, yet fiercely loyal to her husband, her family, and especially her children. She poured her heart and soul into her two sons. Aemelia could name each of their favorite things, from food to music to tutors. She could spot when one was coming down with a cold even before he knew it himself. If either one wasn't in the house, she knew exactly where he liked to play when he was happy, to sulk when he was mad, or to hide when he was crying.

Publius, who had tragically inherited his father's propensity for bouts of illness, was quiet and studious. He, just like Scipio, had fallen in love with Greece. He spent most of his time at home in some odd corner poring through volumes of Greek literature, culture, and history. The time he enjoyed outside was spent imagining he was Socrates questioning a young pupil. The pupil, much to his chagrin, was often his brother, Lucius. Lucius was not studious, though he was obsessed with war stories. He was a young adventurer: athletic, curious, and spending much of his time worrying the various members of the Scipio household with what mischief he was engaging in at that moment. The two boys had become model young men, and Aemelia knew Scipio would be proud.

Yet Aemelia had felt that something was missing. Though her children filled her with overwhelming joy, she felt an emptiness within her while her husband was away. Her salons had dwindled to rare gatherings during which everyone in attendance suggested that they should see one another more often, like they used to. But nothing came of it, and Aemelia was left alone most of her days, wandering from room to room in Villa Scipio. The loneliness grew.

Then, the Galli of Magna Mater came to her door. The Galli had been a modest presence in Rome for a few decades, but as the war intensified, Rome's citizens increasingly turned to gods old and new for protection. The Galli were a group of priests who worshipped a goddess from Anatolia in the east named Cybele, referring to her as Magna Mater, the Great Mother. The Galli lived humble but joyful lives, largely separate from other Romans. Unlike most temple priests, the Galli chose not to become Roman citizens and celebrate the state holidays. But their isolation made them no less joyful. Romans would often pass Galli on the street in their humble gray robes, worn in the feminine fashion, and wonder what they might be laughing about.

Overnight, the Roman people's worship of the goddess Cybele exploded in size, and so did the Galli's influence. The senate even sponsored the temple of Magna Mater as a legitimate place for Roman citizens to worship. As more Romans worshipped there, the Galli began to feel they should embrace their newfound role in Roman society. They decided to visit the houses of the city's preeminent families, which is why Kybe and Aemelia found themselves face-to-face one summer morning.

Kybe had been born in Anatolia, but had been brought to Rome with the Galli as a young orphan. He, along with the rest of the Galli, had made a lifelong pledge to the pursuit of truth. While he conversed with Aemelia in the villa's garden, she could see the earnest sincerity in his eyes. He had a happy mouth and a sweet voice. He listened while she described the anxiety and disappointment that she and her husband had experienced at the hands of Fabius's deceitful disciples. He told her that he knew of her troubles and trusted that her husband was as valiant as she said he was. He also knew how brave she was in her own right.

From that day on, Kybe was Aemelia's friend and confidant. When he was not attending to the temple, he would tutor her children, study the herbs in the garden, or simply stroll through the house and speak with her for hours on end. Their friendship blossomed, and the lonely emptiness that Aemelia felt soon disappeared.

After a long journey across the steep hills and expansive plains that separated Italica from Rome, Laelius and Scipio finally walked the streets of the city. They were followed by a garrison of soldiers transporting a sampling of the spoils from Scipio's victories in Spain, though Scipio insisted on avoiding the pomp of a parade. One would never have guessed the riches that the humble soldiers carried as they traversed the busy streets. But something was off. Though both friends were used to being recognized by the citizens of Rome, the ghoulish looks they received as they strode through the streets was a new extreme. The reactions from passersby made Scipio and Laelius feel as if they were two ghosts who had manifested in broad daylight. Laelius glanced at Scipio, who appeared to him as usual, albeit equally confounded. As the two neared Villa Scipio, both were thoroughly convinced that they had entered a foreign Rome.

Just as they were preparing to enter Scipio's home, a stranger appeared in the doorway. He had Greek features, full lips, and long, dark hair. His overflowing gray cloak hid his feet and gave him the illusion of levitation as he walked. He had kind, understanding eyes augmented by long, black lashes. Upon seeing Scipio, he bowed and greeted him with an enthusiastic "General!"

Scipio's gaze followed the man, who disappeared into the crowd. Their return was becoming more perplexing by the minute. The two men entered the villa.

"Father!"

A young man whom Laelius barely recognized as young Publius ran up to Scipio and wrapped his arms around the general's waist. He had grown into a vibrant youth since Laelius had last seen him. Scipio glowed with pride as he reciprocated his son's embrace.

Aemelia appeared in the courtyard. Her face was pale with shock, but it soon blossomed into immense joy. She ran to her husband, threw her arms around his neck, and kissed him passionately, only letting go of him to give Laelius a chaste kiss on the cheek.

"I told them it wasn't true," Aemelia sighed through happy tears. "I told them, but they kept insisting!"

"What wasn't true?" Scipio asked. "Whom did you tell?"

"Fabius the Younger," Aemelia said, "and the other consuls

in their party. They've been telling everyone that your victories in Spain were all rumor and hyperbole. Some even claimed that you were dead and that another general had taken up command in your name."

The color left Scipio's face. "Rest assured, my love, I am alright."

"He was only sick, but definitely alive," Laelius added. "We thought that the rumors of his death had ended long ago."

"Not here," Aemelia told them, shaking her head. "Fabius's party is the majority in the senate. They spread lies at every turn to undermine you and turn the people of Rome against you."

"Who was that man, the one in the gray cloak? One of Fabius's men?" Scipio asked her.

"Kybe? No, he is a friend," Aemelia said, her face brightening. "He is a priest of the Magna Mater. He believes in truth. He came to comfort me." She cleared her throat and wiped a tear from her cheek. "It has not been easy fighting off the deceit of Fabius's party on my own."

Scipio broke away from his wife, fire blazing in his eyes.

"Where are you going?" she called after him.

"To prove that I am still breathing!" he answered, heading back out the door.

Laelius followed Scipio out of the villa and stood beside him as he directed the rest of the garrison to follow him. They marched through the streets of the city until they came to the stairs of the senate. As luck would have it, Fabius the Younger stood on the steps conversing with another consul. When Fabius laid eyes on Scipio, Laelius noted a shiver of panic streak across the man's face. Scipio stopped at the foot of the steps and faced him.

"General Scipio," Fabius the Younger laughed awkwardly, "I thought you were dead."

Though Fabius the Younger did not agree with his father politically, Laelius had to admit that he preferred the elder's taste in greeting.

Stone-faced, Scipio lifted his arm. On cue, Scipio's soldiers poured fourteen thousand pounds of silver onto the steps of the senate. The other consuls who had gathered stepped back at the initial crash. Those who had followed the march marveled at the riches. Scipio simply stood and stared into Fabius the Younger's eyes. Once the last silver piece had fallen, Scipio opened his mouth.

"Consider this my funeral tribute."

With that, Scipio turned his back, leaving Fabius the Younger blushing hotly.

During the following election cycle, Scipio was elected *pontifex maximus*. The day after his election, he began to speak with consuls privately about the possibility of a siege in Africa. Most were skeptical at first, but many warmed to the idea. Scipio still had some political clout, as well as his unparalleled military record and his unstoppable charm. But Fabius the Younger's party was fierce. They knew that Scipio had a motive for returning to Rome, and it was not long before they too caught wind of the plan to invade Africa. From then on, Scipio was locked in a race against his political competitors. Scipio, unfortunately, was at a disadvantage, being on the offensive. With Hannibal still on Italian soil, it was nearly impossible to shift the senate's focus away from the threat immediately at hand. But Fabius's men did not depend on Hannibal's presence alone. They leaned further into spreading fear of imminent doom among Rome's people, sending whisperers to circulate rumors of Hannibal's increased proximity among the city's foremost gossips and pontificators. They began every forum with overtures about protecting Italy's sovereignty and the importance of domestic stability. They came as close as they could to calling Scipio a traitor for his ambitious plan. But Scipio persisted.

The Galli became ambassadors for Scipio's cause, convincing unwitting consuls that a voyage across the sea might just achieve victory for Rome. This loyalty to Scipio had grown out of Aemelia's friendship with Kybe. Scipio was at first suspicious of his wife's allegiance to the priest, but he soon found Kybe to be a useful ally. The more time Scipio spent speaking with Kybe, the more the young priest trusted Scipio and recommended that the other Galli do so as well. Just as Laelius had been emphatically welcomed into Villa Scipio so many years ago, so too did Kybe swiftly become a beloved member of Scipio's household.

But Scipio's time in the senate was not so enjoyable. The harder he pushed for a campaign against Carthage, the more stubborn the Fabian consuls became. Scipio became frustrated, which only pressed him deeper into political scheming. Family dinners gradually grew briefer as Scipio's strategy meetings with his brother and Laelius encroached on the household's evening meals. Despite her unyielding support of her husband, Aemelia found that Scipio's obsession with politics had made him almost unrecognizable to her. Finally, one night, as Laelius, Lucius, and her husband were pushing aside their plates of untouched fruit yet again, she spoke up.

"My love, have you forgotten yourself?" she exclaimed. Her tone took all three men by surprise, rendering them speechless. "Just a few months ago, you faced a crowd of mutinous men and changed their hearts with your own words. You turned Spanish rebels into allies. You defeated some of Carthage's greatest generals. Surely you can take on a few politicians." She stood defiantly, challenging him.

But Scipio simply glowed with adoration. His wife's undying belief in him had yet again lifted his spirits. He ran to her, lifted her into a spinning embrace, and kissed her passionately.

The next day at the forum, Scipio stood before the senate. Laelius recognized the configuration from before: Fabius Maximus in the center, flanked by the other consuls. Fabius the Younger stood at his father's right hand, looking down upon Scipio. But Scipio stood defiantly as his wife had the night before. The time for whispered strategies and rumors had passed.

"*Mare nostrum*," he began. "That is what we call the Mediterranean: 'our sea.' But she is not 'our' sea, for as it stands, we share her with our enemy. We share her with the people who have overtaken our lands, stolen our resources, and poisoned the minds of our citizens. They have burned down villages and killed our fathers, sons, uncles, nephews, and friends. For generations, we have fought against them, but always on their terms. After every defeat, they sail back across 'our' sea and they plan. They regroup. They attack us again. As long as we allow Carthage to hold the other side of our sea, we will suffer. That is why I propose a campaign against the city of Carthage itself."

Fabius's face hardened into a skeptical scowl.

Scipio looked to Laelius, who nodded encouragingly. He knew Scipio could convince them if he had confidence in himself.

Scipio went on. "Italy has suffered long. It is Carthage's turn to be devastated by fire and sword."

Slowly, like embers crackling into a flame, applause burbled up from those gathered. The consuls whom Scipio had convinced clapped enthusiastically. Kybe and others of the gathered Galli added their applause to the din. The entire forum was filled with whooping and shouts of encouragement until Fabius Maximus stood. All fell silent. A smirk was plastered on Fabius the Younger's face. Scipio stood strong and soldierly before him. Fabius cleared his throat.

"General Scipio, your wisdom and ambition precede you. A campaign such as you suggest is unheard of. Hannibal, Carthage's greatest general, is not in his home city in Africa, but at our doors. Rome is a European city and our concerns are European. Still, your examination of Rome's hold on mare nostrum is true; the sea is what separates us from the bulk of our enemy's fire. That is why I will allow you command of Roman troops in Sicily, the Italian soil most vulnerable to Carthaginian attack."

Scipio's defiant shoulder deflated. A disappointed hush rolled throughout the forum, except for the consuls who sat beside Fabius, who only smiled wider.

"However," Fabius Maximus continued, "should you decide that such a campaign is necessary to ensure Rome's national security, I allow you permission to invade Africa as you see fit."

A murmur rushed throughout the crowd.

"But Father—" Fabius the Younger piped up, turning to Fabius Maximus, distraught.

"My decision is final," Fabius Maximus interrupted. "We are dismissed."

The celebration at Villa Scipio that night was tremendous. Scipio invited all his political allies to feast with them, and the villa's cook did not disappoint. Young Lucius and Publius ran about their home wildly, energized by the strange new faces. Scipio's friends and family cheered, toasted, and sang late into the night. It was a celebration that they would all remember to their dying days.

Laelius, who was seated beside Scipio as usual, drank an excess of wine and felt a bit ill. He stumbled into the garden to get some fresh air. He looked up, and the stars were smiling down on the happy home. As he shakily stood to return to the merriment, his ear picked up a faint conversation in the atrium. He poked his head around the corner, squinting to see in the dim light. Kybe was speaking to Scipio.

"We Galli are not prone to visions, as other worshippers claim," he told the general, "but hearing your speech today, I felt a sudden divine understanding. I am not sure if it was from Magna Mater or some other deity, but I believe I saw a great river, perhaps an ocean. I saw a Roman general such as you crossing the river with an army, and I understood that in doing so, he had set forth an irreversible chain of events. What was the result? Greatness. I saw a Rome that ruled beyond mare nostrum, beyond Spain, even beyond Anatolia. Rome had become the most powerful state in the history of civilization, a mortal Olympus!

"I cannot leave my fellow Galli," Kybe continued, "and I do not think Aemelia could bear it if both of us left her. But the Galli's influence reaches farther than you might suspect. Magna Mater has eyes, ears, and hands working in cities far beyond even your ambitious gaze. Should you need help, do not hesitate to ask for it."

With that, Kybe bowed, kissed Scipio's cheek, and drifted out of the front door.

The day that Scipio and Laelius left for Sicily was a stark contrast to the night of revelry that followed his assignment.

Tears filled Aemelia's eyes more than ever before. Among the three of them, there was a quiet understanding that this good-bye was different from the others. It was commonly understood that Scipio would return to Rome in a hero's chariot or a casket. Scipio bade his wife and sons farewell, and the two friends slowly departed.

Walking toward the gates, Laelius recalled the horrified expressions that had greeted them when they had entered Rome. He prayed it would be the last time he would be treated as a dead soldier entering the city.

Chapter Thirteen

VETERANS AND VOLUNTEERS—205 B.C.

As soon as Scipio landed in Sicily, he began preparations to invade Africa. Though he and Laelius stepped off their boat as night was beginning to fall, he insisted that they unpack their supplies to begin strategizing while the commander's tent was being built around them. Laelius agreed, though he was still somewhat shaken from disembarking the boat.

Scipio had been assigned command of the Fifth and Sixth legions, the subset of the Roman forces who had famously fought against Hannibal and lost at the Battle of Cannae back in 218 B.C. Because their defeat had been so devastating and spectacular, Fabius's party had dismissed them to defend Sicily. While the Italian island was one of the closest points to the Carthaginian mainland, most assumed that after the First War, Carthage would only invade Sicily once they had taken hold of the rest of Italy. Thus, the Fifth and Sixth legions had been banished to this far-off, sleepy post. Scipio suspected that Fabius had done the same to him to keep him out of his hair.

But these men were experienced fighters, veterans who had faced Rome's most powerful enemy head-on. They had seen defeat, but that had only fed their anger and determination. The men of the Fifth and Sixth infantries were raring to fight, tired of the monotony and fragile peace of Sicily. These were men who Scipio understood. These were men he could command.

In fact, Scipio's reputation had preceded him. The morning after their arrival, Scipio and Laelius were greeted by a soldier's feast held by the legions in their honor. The celebration lasted the entire day, including multiple meals, toasts, speeches, performances, salutes, jokes, and even a horse race. The men implored Scipio to compete, and he simply could not resist. He won the race along the beach by a foot. All throughout the celebration, the soldiers told Scipio how thankful they were to have a legitimate military commander in charge. They were bored. They were frustrated. Scipio saw in each admission the ambition and yearning to prove oneself that Scipio knew lay in the heart of every Roman citizen. Though he may not have told Laelius in so many words, Laelius also saw that these men reminded Scipio of how much he yearned for victory.

But his ascension to command was not all smooth sailing. Back in the city, Scipio's enemies were working tirelessly to curtail Scipio's power and ability to invade Africa. A few days after their arrival, Scipio and Laelius received correspondence that they would be given no money for additional troops and therefore could not court mercenary fighters. Though the Fifth and Sixth legions were fierce, they were small. Alone, it would be ridiculous to attempt a siege of Carthage. After tossing the correspondence into the fiery brazier, Scipio and Laelius set about strategizing how to gain volunteer soldiers. The men of the Fifth and Sixth legions provided helpful advice to that end. "Everyone knows Scipio's name in Sicily," many of the men assured the commander. "Greek or Roman, you will have no trouble finding men to fight for you."

By springtime, Scipio had fallen in with the Sicilians. They had certainly heard of Scipio's prowess as a military commander and all but worshipped him. Those who were of appropriate age with financial and physical ability flocked to his army. In no time, Scipio's forces had increased by a third, all volunteer. The adoration was indeed mutual. Sicily had always possessed an eclectic population, mostly mainland Italians and Greek islanders who had sailed to the beautiful southern jewel. Over the generations, the island and its inhabitants had become a unique mix of Greek and Italian fashion, art, culture, and sensibilities. Not even the devastation visited upon the island by the First War had extinguished Sicily's vibrancy. Scipio's childhood love for Greece reignited, and the hospitality and admiration of the local people fed his flames.

Scipio began to dress in Grecian cloaks and slippers as many of the Greek Sicilians did. He dined with Greek families and admired the Grecian art and architecture. When he was not acting as commander, he would stroll about the Sicilian gymnasium and admire the breathtaking view. The sea became more crystal blue every day. The flowers bloomed on the hillside. The world around Scipio shimmered and sparkled like the purest glass. As the days went on, Laelius noticed Scipio speaking less and less of Rome. He treated the correspondences that arrived from the senate as threats from a hostile foreign power. Scipio had found a home away from his beloved Rome. It was as if he had unwittingly stepped into a childhood fantasy.

Scipio seemed deaf to the criticisms that came to Sicily in whispers or between the lines of letters and edicts from Rome.

His grand adoption of Greek fashion and customs had caused many consuls to raise their eyebrows. Scipio was renowned as one of Rome's most loyal leaders, yet he put his feet into Greek slippers every morning and dined with Greek Sicilians every evening. Even through the whispers, Laelius could sense Fabius's party sowing seeds of doubt into the minds of Roman citizens that perhaps their beloved general did not believe in Rome's preeminence after all.

But Laelius knew better. For every afternoon that Scipio spent strolling through the gymnasium in Grecian robes was an early morning that he spent training his troops. Though he only had thirty-two thousand soldiers, marines, and cavalrymen under his command, he trained them to battle as if they were an army twice their size. The men of the Fifth and Sixth legions never doubted Scipio's loyalty to his cause. From sunrise deep into the starlit night, the only thing on Scipio's mind was the invasion of Carthage. Laelius worried about his friend's dedication. At times, he feared that it bordered on obsession. When he first caught wind of the criticisms of his friend's Grecophilia, he wished that Scipio would have enough sense to be subtler, but now Laelius was glad that Scipio had found a respite from the overwhelming pressures of planning the African invasion.

Well into spring, Scipio had garnered volunteers from most of the noble Sicilian families, but his army's weak spot was still its cavalry. A group of noblemen came together and pledged three hundred volunteer Sicilian cavalrymen to Scipio's cause. It was one of the most flattering gestures that Scipio had ever received. But despite the noblemen's generosity, they did not have nearly enough men to stage an attack on Carthage.

One warm evening, Scipio called Laelius into his tent for an emergency meeting. Scipio stood above a brass bowl filled with water, shaving his beard. He ran the blade beneath his chin expertly as Laelius strode in.

"It's the cavalry. It's always the cavalry," Laelius confirmed. "There's no way that the men in our ranks will be able to fight the full force of Carthage's mercenary Numidian horsemen."

Scipio dipped the blade in the water and ran it against his cheek. "What news have we gotten from Massinissa?"

"Always brief and never good," Laelius grumbled, taking a seat. "The last correspondence we received from him confirmed that he is still trying to regain his throne with little more support than he had before. That was when we arrived in Sicily."

"And what about Syphax?"

"Silence," Laelius said stonily. "We continue to send him messages, but have yet to receive any word back."

Scipio hummed disapprovingly and his brow furrowed. His head jerked back as a drop of crimson blood fell from the tip of his chin into the basin. The red droplet spread and turned in the still water. Scipio wiped beneath his chin.

"I believe the time has come to shore up our alliances across the sea." Scipio pressed a cloth to his damp face before throwing it against the side of the basin. "I will take my leave as soon as possible."

Laelius stood. "It will be too dangerous for you to cross the Mediterranean now. Word will have spread about your position in Sicily, and there is no telling what assumptions our enemies might be making about your plans. Besides, your men need you here. They are still training every day and they will need your guidance." Laelius squared his shoulders and faced Scipio. "I will go across the sea."

~

The water was choppy when Laelius's ship landed at Hippo Diarrhytus. He had been able to secure a response from Massinissa that the two would meet at the shore. Many questions floated above the troubled surface of the impending meeting. If Massinissa had not taken back his father's throne, would he still come to Rome's side when their forces crossed the Mediterranean? Where was Syphax, and why was he no longer responding to Scipio's communications? What did the Carthaginians know about Scipio's plan to invade? Did they know that Laelius had disembarked with a small fleet of Romans from Sicily, and would they be lying in wait when they landed? All these questions churned in Laelius's mind as the modest legion cautiously set up camp on the beach. Then, they waited.

Three weeks later, they heard the sound of hooves growing louder. An infantryman spotted Massinissa's men approaching. When Massinissa and his men finally arrived at Laelius's camp, it was clear that he was displeased.

"Carthage knows you're here," Massinissa growled.

"Do they know that we are discussing the invasion?" Laelius asked.

"They think you *are* the invasion," Massinissa barked. "Whispers of a Roman invasion of Africa have been spreading through the area around Carthage like a plague, but most of the Carthaginian nobility dismissed it as rumor. Your landing here has confirmed the rumors, and now Carthage is taking up arms. They are tripling their security and fortifying the city in every way that they can. You have ruined whatever element of surprise existed."

He huffed and stared directly into Laelius's eyes, as if trying to see the cogs turning inside Laelius's head. "Why is he taking so long to invade, anyway?"

"We aren't ready," Laelius explained. "We don't have the manpower. There have been complications with recruiting and limitations from the Roman Senate, and we cannot afford to invade at this point."

"You cannot afford to stay put," Massinissa snapped. "As we speak, a pretender still sits on my father's throne and every day Syphax sends more troops to support him. Your secret siege is no longer secret; every minute that your general stays on that island, our enemies have more time to fortify, more time to garner men and supplies—"

"Syphax is no enemy of Rome," Laelius reminded him. "He is our ally."

Massinissa scoffed. "You have formed an affiliation with an infamous betrayer. If he has not done so already, Syphax will forget your alliance as soon as a more appealing opportunity presents itself. Or worse, he will wait until Scipio is on African soil and turn him over to the Carthaginians," he mused, "but only if he is smart."

Laelius frowned, looking the exiled prince up and down. He gazed beyond Massinissa to his men, lined up soldierly behind him, most on horseback. They stood rigid, steadfast, and loyal as any military men. But they looked tired. Their clothing was worn and showed constant mending. They were thin and their eyes betrayed the desperation of men who lived meal to meal. Even the horses twitched anxiously and impatiently, both fearing and waiting for the next battle.

Laelius imagined who these men must have been in a previous life. Most of them had likely been Numidian nobles or enterprising young men who had sailed across a sea to see a foreign land, fight a few exciting battles, and, if they survived, enjoy the riches and comforts of veteran soldiers. Now they were refugees, forced into a lean and nomadic existence. Even their commander, whom Laelius knew would be followed by these men to their graves, looked at Laelius with desperation beneath his indignation. They needed a profound change to their situation. They needed Rome to invade.

Laelius was thinking about how he could assure Massinissa that the invasion was on its way without making promises that he could not keep, given the status of Scipio's forces, when a shout alerted Laelius from the camp. He turned and realized that most of the fleet was looking out to sea. A Roman ship was approaching. Laelius and Massinissa, who was clearly displeased at yet another Roman ship alerting the Carthaginians to Rome's plans, met the ship on the shore. A messenger disembarked and immediately ran to Laelius, nearly out of breath.

"Sir," he said, "the general requests your immediate return to Sicily. There has been some turmoil in Locri."

Chapter Fourteen

TROUBLE IN LOCRI—204 B.C.

L ocri was a small town just at the tip of the Italian boot. As in many small southern Italian villages, its inhabitants led lives separate from the Roman city's populace. Few had ever even seen the city, though the townspeople of Locri would adamantly agree that they were Roman citizens. But after the Battle of Cannae, the town fell into Carthaginian hands. For eleven years, Carthaginian soldiers had occupied the town, though they left the lives of the Locrians largely uninterrupted. The Locrians became used to seeing the foreign soldiers and paying the increased taxes. Deep within their hearts, they yearned to have control turned back to Rome, but little had changed for the townspeople day to day.

Then Scipio arrived in Sicily. Across the Messina Strait, the Carthaginians who controlled Locri became nervous and began to tighten their grip on the town. They stripped the freedoms of the townspeople, instituting curfews and rationing the food they farmed or hunted. They became hostile and began to beat upstarts and insubordinates in the streets. The simple life the Locrians had known became filled with violence, hunger, and fear. So a trio of men exiled themselves from the town in an attempt to garner help for their situation. They found Scipio.

As Scipio described to Laelius upon the latter's arrival back in Sicily, the trio of exiles appeared in the camp one evening. They appealed to Scipio, imploring him to help their cause. They believed that, left uninhibited, the Carthaginians would destroy the town. They had even received word that Hannibal was on his way to the town to set fire to their beloved Temple of Proserpina himself.

Scipio could hardly resist the chance to face Hannibal in battle. After consulting with a few other generals, he agreed to defend the town of Locri and liberate it from the Carthaginians. The men in his legion had been training diligently and were itching for battle. Scipio gathered his troops and marched them just to the outskirts of the town, where Carthaginian sentries would not detect them. When Hannibal's army arrived at the town, Scipio lay in waiting. He watched Hannibal speak with a few of the occupying generals. The man beamed with just as much confidence and authority as he had when Scipio had last seen him at Cannae. At one point, Hannibal and the Carthaginian generals disappeared, and Scipio's generals determined that they must have gone into the town. Once night had fallen, Scipio gave the order to attack the town under cover of darkness.

Scipio's forces surprised the Carthaginian sentries and swiftly infiltrated the city. All of Scipio's men fought valiantly, floored by the opportunity to finally fight. The new skills that they had mastered through Scipio's training were executed beautifully. But once the battle had finished and the dust had settled, Scipio looked around and realized that Hannibal was nowhere to be found. Scipio walked to the outskirts of the town and found nothing. Hannibal's army had left. Vexed and frustrated, Scipio returned to his men in town and was presented with a young, scrawny Carthaginian infantryman who had surrendered himself to Scipio's legion as a messenger.

"General Hannibal has taken his leave," the messenger hissed at Scipio. "He does not wish to waste his men on an unworthy adversary."

"And so I returned to Sicily," Scipio told Laelius. His weary visage, the shadows beneath his eyes, and the wrinkles around his face were accentuated by the shadows cast by the flaming brazier. He gazed across at Laelius and his eyes grew sad. "I'm loath to admit it, but Hannibal's provocation got to me. That very night I set out a plan to escalate the timeline of the invasion. I wanted him to feel the pain," Scipio said darkly, "the pain of having an army dangle your home over the precipice of destruction, as he had done with Locri. I wanted to waste no time. That morning, I made preparations to immediately leave Locri and return to the camp to begin instituting my new plan."

Scipio huffed and stared off toward the horizon. The waves rose and crashed peacefully onto the sandy shore. The music of the sea billowed up the mountainside along with the salty sea air, filling the tent. Scipio's breathing slowed and his eyes filled with regretful memory. He sighed and turned back to Laelius.

"In my haste, I failed to properly establish leadership in Locri. The Locrians desperately yearned to be rejoined to Rome, but much has happened in eleven years. They required someone to fill the hole that the Carthaginians left. So, when Pleminius volunteered to stay behind and take charge, I allowed it without a second thought."

Scipio ran a hand through his hair. "A few weeks later, the reports began to come to Sicily. Men who had been left to serve under Pleminius wrote of him plundering the city and hording the resources for his garrison. They claimed that he had tortured Carthaginian sympathizers, first quietly under the cover of night and then out in public in full daylight. He has been exerting absolute power over the garrison meant to welcome the Locrians back into Rome's arms and, on top of this, reports have started to arrive that he has been disparaging my name. Now the soldiers trapped at Locri are looking to me to help them. In Rome, Fabius's party is enjoying this immensely, of course! They can spin the whole situation any way they please: Either I'm an incompetent commander or a sadistic beast! Had I known that he was a completely power-hungry maniac, of course I never would have considered—" Scipio stopped. He was shouting now and breathing heavily. He calmed and recomposed himself. "The final blow came this morning when Pleminius raided the Temple of Proserpina."

Like many southern Italian towns, Locri worshipped its own lesser gods alongside the gods of the Roman state. Proserpina was the protector of Locri. The Locrians prayed to and bestowed offerings and sacrifices upon her to provide the town with a plentiful harvest, healthy newborns, peaceful deaths, and freedom from disease and warfare. When their ancestors established Locri, long before anyone could remember— when farmland was cleared away, houses erected, and walls built to protect the townspeople—Locri's matriarchs brought Proserpina inside the walls of the town with them. They built a magnificent temple for their goddess, one so glorious and ornate that it quickly became renowned throughout all of Italy. For generations, Locrians would present special meals, bushels of grain from the harvest, and baskets of fruit at the feet of the goddess's effigy inside the temple. They began every holiday and celebration at the temple's doors. The Temple of Proserpina was the Locrians' most incredible achievement and the greatest gift they had to pass down to their children.

By the time that word of Pleminius's raid of the temple reached Scipio, violence had already erupted in the streets of Locri. The Locrians refused to have the greatest monument to their beloved goddess tarnished. Violence begat more violence and Pleminius responded with deadly military precision. Pleminius instituted stricter curfews and restrictions on the townspeople than the Carthaginians ever had. Any Locrian who disobeyed an order was dragged into the streets and humiliated before the public.

Plundering the Temple of Proserpina was not only an egregious act, but also a blasphemous one. Acts of blasphemy and sacrilege were some of the most serious offenses in the eyes of the Roman Senate, tantamount to treason, for a betrayal of the sanctity of the gods was a betrayal of the state as well. Laelius carefully read over the charge of impiety that had been delivered to Scipio's camp from the senate. They certainly did not hesitate to implicate Scipio in Pleminius's crimes.

"We have to try him in Locri for his crimes," Laelius concluded. "If we send him to Rome, they will find a way to tie you into all of it."

Scipio shook his head. "There is no way for them to do that."

"They'll find a way," Laelius insisted. "Once they have Pleminius, they'll get him to confess that he was acting under orders, or they'll use his trial to throw suspicion on you. Scipio, you know Fabius. You know that they don't care about Pleminius. They're trying to get to you."

"But the charge clearly says that the senate *wishes* to try Pleminius in Rome."

"Yes, the senate wishes. But you are the commander. You choose. If you decide that his crimes do not warrant a trial in Rome, you may judge him for yourself."

Scipio was worried. His jaw tightened. "Fine. We will try him in Locri."

"My husband was dragged into the streets by two Roman soldiers and beaten until blood flowed from his lips like water."

The small Locrian woman who spoke before the justice council did not have the slightest trepidation in her eyes. She sat with a confidence that Laelius never would have expected a farmer's wife to possess in front of a consul, especially not one of Scipio's renown. Scipio merely listened to her testimony, expressionless yet kind, as he had for countless others over the past weeks.

"When I got him back," the woman continued, "I barely recognized him—my husband! He was defending our people against tyranny, the worst we have ever suffered. He was defending Proserpina."

Pleminius had been swiftly apprehended by the forces that Scipio and Laelius had brought with them. Most of Pleminius's followers immediately reoriented themselves to Scipio's side, begging for mercy. The Locrians were also enthused to see Pleminius arrested, though they were also notably more skeptical than celebratory of Scipio's return. Pleminius's trial was held in the town's central forum. There was no escaping the disruption that the trial caused in the Locrians' day-to-day activities, but if nothing else, justice was to be served.

The trials had been an endless parade of testimonies from Locrians and men who served under Pleminius detailing the various atrocities that he had committed. Despite the justice council's best efforts to limit the witnesses' testimonies to events around the raiding of the Temple of Proserpina, those testifying could not help but include every detestable action and reaction that Pleminius had set in motion. With each despicable tale, Laelius could see Scipio even more weighed down with guilt. Despite the general's commanding exterior, Laelius saw regret every time he looked into his friend's weary eyes.

The next testifier entered the forum, also possessing a distinctly confident stride. Most women from small towns whom Laelius had encountered were prone to shyness when faced with authority, but she faced the justice council with masculine energy. She had fair and lovely features, and it seemed to Laelius that he had seen her somewhere before. From the way that Scipio leaned forward, Laelius could tell that he had the same impression.

"Begin whenever you are ready," Scipio told her, "though we would like to remind you that this tribunal's sole concern is the accused's actions concerning the Temple of Proserpina."

"That will be no problem," she said clearly, "for my entire life has revolved around the temple. I have been an attendant of Proserpina since I was very young. She has always protected me and given me strength, as she has most of this town. Proserpina gives our people life, and we give life to her." The woman smiled thoughtfully. "The gods cannot exist without our faith in them. What Pleminius has done is unacceptable. To disrespect a god as he has is to invite absolute ruin!"

Her face grew shadowed as she continued. "Proserpina's domain is harvest and plenty—without her, our crops would die, our livestock would have nothing to eat, and we would all starve. We have known so many changes over the years . . . over the past weeks, even. But never have we feared for our home as much as we have under General Pleminius. Never before have we feared so much—yes, for our husbands and our leaders, but also for our souls. Without Proserpina's blessing, Locri would be nothing but infertile dirt. Troy was one of the greatest cities in the world when it fell out of the gods' favor, and look what happened to it. Imagine how our small town would fare."

She turned to Scipio abruptly, looking directly into his eyes. "You have spoken often that we are all Romans, but you in the city care little for our gods. You call them 'lesser,' preferring the grandeur of Jupiter, Mars, and Neptune. But these gods are our home. They are what make us Roman. Do not dismiss us for that, and do not dismiss this man's sacrilege because he spurned a 'lesser' goddess."

"Do not worry," Scipio retorted. "Justice will be served."

The woman nodded knowingly. "Yes, I'm sure it will be. I'm sure the gods will serve their justice, which is the truest justice, but what will you do?"

After the woman had left, Scipio called for a recess and pulled Laelius aside.

"I have decided to send Pleminius to Rome," Scipio said. "That is the right thing to do."

"But—"

"After all I have heard over these weeks, Pleminius has wronged these people more than I could have imagined. They deserve for their tormentor to have a full trial in the city."

Laelius nodded, though his frustration was evident. Scipio

patted his shoulder and went to inform the rest of the justice council of his intentions.

As Laelius left the forum, he caught a glimpse of the woman who had testified walking swiftly down the road. He could not shake the feeling that he somehow knew her, though he could not say why. He became determined to find out.

Laelius followed her down an alley and onto the next street. He pursued her secretly as she wound through the town of Locri. It was as if she were worried that someone might follow her. At some point, she spoke with a merchant briefly and received a heavy gray fabric from him.

Eventually, she left the town, carrying the fabric in both arms, and walked into the woods just outside of Locri. Laelius continued to pursue her as she floated from tree to tree. Every once in a while she would drop a piece of jewelry, like gifts for the woods. She also appeared to be getting taller and broader. The chase was so enchanting that Laelius could not help but go on despite his better judgment. Who was this woman?

Then, she shed the braid that had been tied around the crown of her head. When Laelius came to it, he found it to be horsehair. Soon after, she donned the gray fabric, and Kybe, the Gallus of Magna Mater, stood before him. Kybe swiftly floated away, either ignorant or indifferent to Laelius's presence.

Questions flooded Laelius's mind. The entire experience was altogether so spectacular and strange that once Laelius returned to the normalcy of Locri, he completely forgot to tell Scipio about it until Kybe appeared to them again much later.

With Pleminius on his way to Rome to be tried by the senate, Laelius and Scipio returned to Sicily. When they arrived back at camp, a message was waiting for Scipio from Syphax. The plans had changed. Syphax was a married man now.

Chapter Fifteen

A CHANGE OF DIRECTION—204 B.C.

The envoy had arrived the day before Laelius and Scipio returned to Sicily. Laelius recognized the messenger from Syphax's court. He had seen the young man in the halls of the palace. Evidently, Syphax recognized that this message was of some importance, or else he would have not have sent a soldier so close to him across the sea. Then again, Laelius wondered, was it possible that he was yet another of Syphax's clever manipulations, a friendly face to soften the blow of the news?

No amount of cleverness could cover the plain facts: A few weeks ago, Syphax had married the daughter of Hasdrubal Gisgo. She was called Saphanba'al, famous across northern Africa for her incredible beauty and sharp wit. According to the messenger, Hasdrubal Gisgo had brought her to dine with him and Syphax at Syphax's palace and the Numidian king was struck down with infatuation. The courtship lasted only days. By the time it was over, Syphax was all but groveling at her father's feet for her hand.

Saphanba'al's father did not grant his daughter's hand without requiring recompense from Syphax. Syphax was now tied to Carthage both matrimonially and politically, which naturally complicated his relationship with Scipio and his invading army. Never one to burn a bridge until he had pillaged the other end's resources completely, Syphax sent an envoy to Scipio to renegotiate the terms of their friendship. As the messenger reported every detail of Syphax's betrayal, his words dripped with a condescending, syrupy optimism, as if Scipio would simply shrug his shoulders at the news and wish Syphax congratulations for the wedding.

The messenger finished by informing Scipio, "My king wishes to assure you that he remains Rome's ally. He wishes no ill will upon the Roman state or the Imperator himself."

Scipio's jaw tightened. After all these years, he still hated that term.

The messenger's eyes twinkled. "In fact, my king sees his marriage as an opportunity for further unification. Syphax, of course, will not betray his father-in-law and therefore cannot condone General Scipio's current plan to invade the city of Carthage. He hopes that General Scipio will consider a less violent and extremist alternative—a peace, even, between himself and Carthage. Even if the Roman state refuses to act with friendship toward Carthage, perhaps the General will. My king assures the General that he and his new father-in-law can offer an extremely enviable reward for such an arrangement."

It was clear from Scipio's expression that he did not take the enticement well, and the messenger's positive attitude faltered beneath Scipio's fiery gaze.

The messenger cleared his throat. "In any case, my king implores General Scipio not to sail to Africa. He will find no friends there if he arrives Carthage's enemy—only fire and despair."

"Go back to your king," Scipio directed the envoy. "Tell him that if he returns to this camp, he will find no friends here."

The messenger sighed, though Syphax had obviously warned him to expect such a response. After all, his entire proposal was insulting to Scipio's intelligence and experience as a leader. So the messenger spoke again, as Syphax had directed him to once Scipio denied his absurd proposal.

"The minute that General Scipio sets foot on African soil, his alliance with my king will be broken completely. His army, which he assures you outnumbers the General's forces, will become hostile to Rome and all of its allies, European or African." The messenger's voice dipped threateningly. "The wandering prince Massinissa's ragtag army will be crushed instantly by our army. My king assures you of that."

"Be gone from my sight," Scipio barked, "and take your king's shallow assurances with you! Give your king *my* assurance that Rome will triumph without the aid of a disloyal ally."

With that final word, Scipio returned to his tent with Laelius in tow. He immediately started laying out his maps of Africa and studying his battle diagrams.

Laelius watched as Scipio quietly skittered throughout the tent from one end to the other, and then back to his plans. After a few minutes he paused and pursed his lips thoughtfully. Laelius had always thought it best not to interrupt his friend when he was deep in thought, but at this particular moment, he worried that Scipio was shielding something within by keeping busy. He decided to speak.

"I presume you won't want to tell the men of Syphax's betrayal."

"Not immediately, no," Scipio muttered. "It would only discourage them, slow them down, and time is of the essence."

"And why is that?"

Scipio turned to Laelius as if he had asked a stupid question with an obvious answer. "We're moving up the timeline of the invasion. We will prepare to set sail in the next few weeks."

"Do you think that's wise?"

"Syphax knows too much about our strategy. I blame myself for allowing him the amount of information on our plan of attack that I did, but there's no going back now. With him allied with the Carthaginians across the sea and the Locri incident fresh in the minds of the Roman senators, we have to act fast before our enemies on either of those fronts decide to try and stop us! One decree from Rome or one well-placed fleet along the African shoreline, and everything—absolutely everything—that we have worked toward here will be for naught!" Scipio was shouting now across the small space in the tent. As the last words left his lips, a silence rang between the two friends.

"Syphax's betrayal was not your fault, Scipio," Laelius ventured.

Scipio turned away. "It doesn't matter now."

"Scipio, we don't need Syphax. The rate at which our men have been progressing, the way that you've been training them—"

"Then why did we place any trust in him in the first place?" Scipio snapped. He huffed and stood at the entrance to the tent, looking out beyond the sea. The slow-moving clouds reflected in his sleep-deprived eyes. "We trust too much, only to be set back. I should have seen this coming. I should have."

Laelius sighed and placed a hand on Scipio's shoulder. "We

need allies. If we are going to defeat the Carthaginians in their own land, we'll need help. But we've come much farther than we anticipated in so little time."

"If Rome learns that Syphax has turned to the Carthaginians, they will never let us cross the sea."

"Then we will prepare to set sail before that happens. We will reach out to Massinissa. We will garner all the support we can. We'll use this setback to our advantage."

Though Scipio nodded and returned to the tent, Laelius felt more distance from his friend than he ever had before. In the quiet of the tent, the two began to strategize as the sun sank below the horizon.

Laelius, Scipio, and his generals spent the next few weeks laying out the plans for an accelerated timeline of the legion's siege of Carthage. Should they attack now, Scipio's army would only have the manpower they currently possessed. They would have to end their volunteer recruitment immediately to get their most recently acquired soldiers up to speed. The cavalry was the legion's weakest point, and without Syphax's army to bolster it, some of the men would have to be retrained as cavalry. They would have to depend on Massinissa to bring experienced horsemen to battle.

As their date of departure neared, their main topic of discussion became where to land the fleet once the legion reached Africa. Initially, they had prepared to dock at Emporiae, south of Thapsus. Scipio had coordinated their location along with Syphax and Massinissa. It had been one of the only details that the two warring Numidian princes could agree on. Emporiae was perfectly situated near enough to Syphax's kingdom to immediately join with his army once Scipio's forces landed, as well as being directly in line with the city of Carthage. But since the alliance with Syphax had broken, proximity became a hindrance rather than an advantage.

"There are a multitude of areas of disembarkation along the coast," General Claudius insisted, tracing his finger over the golden-brown rendering of the African shoreline laid atop Scipio's table. "We will have to choose one that will give us enough distance from both Carthage and Syphax so that neither will attack our fleet. Both will likely be on guard, even with our accelerated schedule."

"We also have to ensure that they won't attack Massinissa when he meets us. Syphax has already threatened him directly," Laelius reminded Claudius.

"The decision is yours, General," Claudius said.

Laelius watched the thoughts tumble through Scipio's mind. He wished that he could decipher the journey that played across the micro-expressions in Scipio's strong features. Scipio had been putting off this decision for weeks and even now he appeared to be grappling with a variety of options.

Finally, Scipio concluded, "We will not divert from our original plans. We will keep the landing site at Emporiae."

Laelius and Claudius exchanged looks, unsure of how to react.

"General—" Claudius began, but Scipio had begun to roll up the map and continue on to another of the many details that still had to be solidified within the new strategy.

"You are dismissed, Claudius."

"General Scipio, this doesn't make any sense—" Laelius tried.

"Dismissed," Scipio insisted, looking up from the map he was unfurling.

It was the look in his eyes, not his dismissal, that stopped Laelius from pushing anymore. Scipio had the same look of wisdom that he always did when he had a secret plan. The thoughts were still tumbling in his mind. Claudius shook his head and left the tent. Laelius stayed, awaiting an explanation that, for whatever reason, Scipio could not reveal to Claudius, but instead Scipio began to discuss the map he had laid out. Whatever scheme Scipio was concocting, Laelius was not allowed access to it, either.

The bright spring sunlight reflected off the morning waves as the Fifth and Sixth legions boarded the vessels that would carry them across the Mediterranean Sea. Over the past few months, the legions had ballooned in size with the influx of Sicilian volunteers. Scipio's men loaded hundreds of pounds of weaponry, metalsmithing tools, food, and fresh water onto the ships. These provisions would have to sustain the army throughout their voyage as well as their siege. The hulls of the ships that carried the army's horses had to be specially built to transport its equestrian passengers. The horses were guided onto these ships and carefully secured into place alongside hundreds of pounds of hay and barley.

A large crowd of Sicilians gathered to watch the fleet set sail. Laelius stood beside Scipio as he oversaw the final preparations. Scipio wore his Sicilian sandals and had styled his robe in the Sicilian fashion, as usual. The crowd seemed equally awestruck by Scipio's army's dutiful work and massive ships as they were by the man himself. Laelius could hear their hushed conversations floating toward him on the sea breeze.

General Claudius came up behind Scipio and spoke

hurriedly into his ear. "Rumors have been circulating of our landing south of Thapsus. If any of Syphax's spies are gathered in this crowd, they will see that we are still headed that way. We must change course!"

"We are staying the course," Scipio said simply before ascending aboard his ship. He waved to the crowd, who began to cheer for him. His men gathered around and stood beneath.

"May Neptune bless our voyage," Scipio announced, "and may Fortuna smile upon our endeavors!"

The crowd of civilians and soldiers applauded as Scipio disappeared into the ship with his brother, Lucius, in tow.

Laelius made his way onto his own vessel, captained by a soldier named Cato. Scipio had assured Laelius that Cato was the smoothest sailor that the army had at their disposal, and Laelius was glad of that.

As they pushed off the shore and steered into the open sea, Laelius's troublesome thoughts distracted him from his aversion to water travel. Scipio must have realized, he surmised, the recklessness of his decisions and the danger he put himself and his army in by allowing the enemy to know their landing site. What was more, he had barely taken the time to wish Laelius a good voyage personally. In fact, they hadn't spoken much as friends since they had returned from Locri. Syphax's betrayal had dealt a harder blow to Scipio than Laelius had expected. Scipio had become more reserved and contemplative than ever. Those thoughts that he would usually confide to Laelius were locked tightly in his mind. Whatever Scipio's plans might be, Laelius barely had an inkling, and this scared him even more than what lay ahead in Africa.

"Sir," Cato called to Laelius.

Laelius wobbled toward the ship's captain. They had pulled

up along the left side of the fleet in line with Scipio and Lucius, who led the right side.

"Sir, we're receiving directions from the commander's ship to change direction. Our landing destination has apparently been changed," said Cato.

"Do as they direct," Laelius said, heaving a sigh of relief.

He realized Scipio had been planning this all along. It made much more sense to change direction mid-voyage, especially with Syphax's spies lurking on land and the large crowd that watched them disembark toward Thapsus. Laelius looked out beyond the horizon, yet still his heart was heavy. The sun beat down on his brow. If only he had known, all of his worries and doubts would have dissipated. If only Scipio had trusted him.

Chapter Sixteen

ATTACK ON THE TOWER CITY—204 B.C.

The fog lay thick and heavy all around Laelius's ship. The sun was hardly visible, and the heavy cover made the day as dark as twilight. The wind whispered in his ear like a phantom, and dark shapes drifted in and out of sight just beyond the bow. They had been sailing for two days, and Cato assured Laelius that they were drawing near the promontory of Mercury. Laelius wondered how the captain could measure distance at all through the oppressive fog that had enveloped them that morning. Even the sea had sunken into a hushed quiet. The men on the ship dared not raise their voices, either. They had entered a foreign land, and Laelius could feel the influence of spirits more ancient than any of Rome's gods.

Soon, the dark rocks became more frequent, and it wasn't long until one of the men spotted the shore. Cato expertly steered the ship around the menacing, bone-white sea stones that towered as high as three men above Laelius's head. Through the mist, he could just see the edge of the cape that encircled the promontory. The men whispered among themselves as Cato guided the ship west of the cape toward the nearest headland. As the view of land became clearer, so did the anticipation of the battles to come. Everything that these men had trained for appeared more real by the minute. All the talk of sailing across the great sea was behind them, for now they had done it. They had made it to Africa.

Cato anchored the ship on the westernmost edge of the beach, and Laelius watched the rest of the flotilla follow suit. As the fog-obscured daylight transitioned to dusk, Laelius disembarked his ship and made his way to Scipio's. Walking along the sandy banks felt like walking through a dream. The white mist curled around his ankles and elbows while the tide nipped at the soles of his feet. Laelius imagined that this was how it felt to walk through the streets of Mount Olympus: slow, timeless, and utterly quiet. When he climbed aboard Scipio's ship, Scipio and Lucius were already deep into strategizing.

"We can set up camp in the Bagradas Valley," Lucius was saying, "which would be the perfect place for Massinissa to meet us."

Scipio turned to Laelius. "Have we heard any word from him? Any news of recent victories, his movements, his men, the numbers we might expect from him when he arrives?"

"None that I know of," Laelius said.

"And," Scipio continued cautiously, "we are sure that Syphax has not sent forces to pursue him?"

"I cannot say anything for sure," Laelius admitted, "but I believe that if Massinissa had met his demise, we would know about it."

"We will find out in a few days, then," Scipio sighed.

"And you are confident in our first move being an advance on Utica?" Lucius confirmed.

"Certainly," Scipio said, his entire presence taking on a lively glow against the mist. "One hundred years ago, the great Roman general Agathocles of Syracuse landed upon this very shore and advanced upon the city of Utica. He built a magnificent tower in his name at the center of the city, and it stood as a wonder of the world for decades. We are his descendants and his kinsmen. We will reclaim that monument and that city in the name of Rome. Not only will Utica provide us with the ideal strategic base for our siege of Carthage, but the Tower of Agathocles will be our first victory across the sea. It will symbolize more for the Republic than any triumph short of marching through the streets of Carthage."

The determination with which Scipio outlined the army's plan filled Laelius with a great deal of hope—so much so that after Scipio dismissed the meeting, Laelius wanted to stay with him and talk deep into the night. He had forgotten how intoxicating Scipio's confidence and belief in a mission could be. However, before Laelius could reach him, Scipio began speaking with the man who had captained his ship. Laelius stayed for a few minutes until Lucius suggested he get some rest. Lucius would be suggesting that Scipio do the same very soon.

As Laelius strolled back to his ship, the silver moonlight sliced through the thick fog, transfiguring the beach into a frosted meadow. Looking out upon the strange, glittering landscape, Laelius could feel the hope still fresh in his heart blooming.

At first light, Scipio's army disembarked from their ships. The fog had dissipated, leaving behind a harsh white sun. Hundreds of infantryman, cavalrymen, horses, and supplies spilled out onto the beach. Scipio and his generals stood at the front of the army. Once the ships had been emptied, the men began to march. They marched for a few days through the mountains and river valleys of northern Africa until they came upon the Bagradas Valley. The valley, which lay just outside the gates of the city of Utica, mainly comprised sleepy farmland. Scipio's army set up a temporary camp and waited for Massinissa to arrive.

It did not take long for the prince's forces to appear. Laelius was shocked by what he saw. Though he had last characterized Massinissa's followers as haggard and exhausted by their long exile, these forces approached the Roman camp with renewed vigor. He could once again see why these men were famed as some of the deadliest horsemen across the Mediterranean. Two hundred experienced Numidian cavalrymen quickly situated themselves among the Roman soldiers, and Laelius could feel his hope growing.

Massinissa was markedly more cautious. Laelius's eyes followed the Numidian patriarch as he paced about Scipio's tent. Laelius's eyes darted to Scipio, who was doing the same.

"These two hundred are all that I have," Massinissa growled, more to himself than to Scipio. "Syphax's men have chased us all across Numidia, neither allowing us to rest nor strategize a counteroffensive against them."

"They appear in much better condition than when I last left you," Laelius said.

"When you last left me, you were not accompanied by the Great Imperator," Massinissa said, turning to Scipio. "Your presence has power over even my men. You resurrect their spirits, General. You have given us a priceless gift: a reason to continue on." Massinissa looked away bashfully. "I only wish I had the power to grant you a gift so liberating."

"I assure you, what you have done for us already is enough," Scipio told him. "Your men are great fighters. I know that they will rise to the occasion when the time comes."

"That occasion may come sooner than you anticipated," Massinissa warned, a shadow passing over his face. "Carthage has sent General Hanno to defend Utica."

Scipio furrowed his brow. They had worried that with Syphax feeding Carthage all he knew of Rome's plans for invasion, Carthage might surmise that Utica would be Scipio's first target. They had considered searching for another location to house their base, but Scipio had decided that the reclamation of the Tower of Agathocles was too important.

"Hanno is stationed at Salaeca, just a stone's throw from the city's walls," said Massinissa. "If he senses even the slightest indication of an attack, he will lock down the city. Carthage has given him a new cavalry force of four thousand to defend it. Do we have the manpower to take on a force that large?"

Laelius certainly did not think so, but Scipio nodded stoically.

"What we lack in numbers we will make up for in spirit," Scipio concluded. "I have nothing but confidence in these men. I have trained them for months. I have broken bread with them. Your cavalry, Massinissa, is famed for its discipline and ruthlessness. If we act wisely, Fortuna will smile upon us in the end." He thought for a moment. "Take your men to Salaeca," he instructed Massinissa. "Engage Hanno there. Hanno is prepared for us to attack Utica, not him. If it does not cripple his troops completely, it will distract him while our main forces head to Utica. In fact . . . ." Scipio's eyebrows knitted together, and Laelius could see the ideas sparking throughout his mind yet again. "Draw out Hanno's forces. If we divide our energy between defeating him and Utica, we may stretch ourselves too thin. But if we concentrate our combined strength on overpowering Hanno, then there will be little to stop us from stepping through the gates of Utica."

Within the next few days, Scipio dispatched Massinissa's forces. As they marched to provoke Hanno's army, Scipio led the Roman forces up out of the valley and into the mountains behind Utica. Laelius caught a glimpse of the city in the distance and the great tower that sprung up at its center. He saw Scipio watching the city as well, a glint of hunger in his eyes. Laelius could not help but notice some pain in his expression, like the face of a once-dear friend that one had not seen in many years. It reminded Laelius of the look in his mother's eyes when he first returned home from the war. Scipio wanted desperately to reclaim the tower.

The Roman army lay in wait, eyes focused on the wide-open valley below. As the sun arced high in the sky, Laelius spotted Massinissa's men riding into the valley. At first, he feared that the horsemen were retreating, but he soon realized that Massinissa had surrounded Hanno. The Carthaginian army poured into the valley, pursued by Numidian cavalry at all sides. With a great whoop, Scipio's army surged down the mountain and into the valley. The Carthaginians were clearly shocked. They greatly outnumbered the Fifth and Sixth legions, but this was the moment for which Scipio's men had prepared. Sicilian noblemen who had never fought on horseback before swiftly cut down

Hanno's cavalry. Seasoned veterans fought alongside volunteers who had never wielded a sword against a Carthaginian soldier. Laelius witnessed a battlefield full of allies, all of whom had been betrayed, ousted from the land they called home, and were hungry to prove themselves. But what was more, he witnessed a field of Carthaginian soldiers more terrified than he had ever seen. If this army were defeated, Hanno could not retreat across a sea. They were battling a few days' march from their beloved city. Hanno's men fought to desperately defend, but Scipio's men fought with the strength of a people who had been defending their homes for generations.

Laelius caught sight of General Hanno, looking frantically about from atop his horse. Laelius galloped in his direction and their swords clashed. Hanno's horse uttered a piercing whinny and took off into the tempest of warring men. Laelius turned to pursue him, but a bronze streak shot past him. Scipio was locked on Hanno, his armor glinting in the noon sun. He sideswiped the Carthaginian leader with his weapon and sent him tumbling to the ground.

Seeing their general bested was likely the final straw for the swiftly diminishing Carthaginian forces. The rest of the men who had the strength to do so retreated, pursued by a few cavalrymen not yet ready to give up the fight. Scipio handed Hanno off to Lucius, who brought him back to camp. The battle had ended. Scipio had claimed his first victory across the sea.

The following day, Scipio moved the Roman camp to the spot where Hanno had set up camp in Salaeca, and turned his attention back to Utica. With Hanno out of the way, Scipio saw nothing to impede his siege of the Tower City. As soon as his army had regrouped, the dead had been honored and buried, and the men had taken time to sufficiently celebrate their victory, Scipio began the march on the city.

Approaching Utica from the land, the first thing that Laelius saw was the wall made of white stone that encircled the city. The hot sun reflected off the stone, turning the wall into a blinding force field. The second thing that drew Laelius's attention was the vague shape of the tower that loomed beyond the wall. When they reached ground level, Laelius could see that the Tower of Agathocles had fallen into ruin. Huge sections of the stone monument had fallen away after nearly a century of neglect. The Numidians who inhabited Utica had shown the structure no love and allowed it to fade. The impressive Roman artifact that Scipio had expected to greet the army was little more than a crumbling reminder of a long-forgotten expedition.

Laelius looked to Scipio, who also gazed up at the towering ruin. His pained expression quickly turned into a fiery determination. He gave the order and the siege began.

Chapter Seventeen

BURNING THE CAMPS—204 B.C.

More than a month after it had started, the siege of Utica was still raging. The Phoenician city's walls had refused to yield to the Romans. The anticipation and thirst for glory that thrust Scipio's men into battle on the first day had settled into an exhausted and frustrated push and pull that felt more like a habit than anything else. Just a few days after the Romans had begun their attack, Syphax and Hasdrubal's combined armies had set up camp in the path between Utica and Carthage. Should the Romans eventually take the city of Utica, their future prospects of transporting the army looked bleak.

The drawn-out siege of the city weighed down the men's morale every day. Though Laelius never once caught wind of mutinous words slipping from the soldiers' lips, he could see in their carriage and in the way they regarded their commander that their hope in Scipio was gradually dying. What was worse, Scipio's own brilliant hope seemed to be suffering as well. When he and Scipio strategized with the other generals, he would catch the commander staring up at the crumbling tower on the other side of the city's wall. At first Laelius saw injustice and rage in Scipio's gaze, but as the days passed, this softened into sadness and mourning. In Scipio's eyes, Laelius saw the whole history of Rome's failures reflected, slowly crumbling into dust and sand. For weeks, generals came to Scipio warning of decreasing provisions and the need for more manpower, but it was the drought of hope that Laelius knew would be the death of their campaign, and so he emboldened himself to take action.

Forty days after the siege had begun, Laelius confronted Scipio following one of their strategy meetings with the other generals.

"We have to retreat," Laelius said firmly.

Scipio did not look back at him, instead continuing to carefully replace his father's maps in the chest where they lived.

Laelius pressed on. "Winter is coming. We barely have the resources to sustain an ongoing siege in summer conditions, let alone the winter. We will have to withdraw and set up a base closer to the coast so that we can send for more supplies from Sicily. When the spring returns, we may be able to continue where we left off, which won't be much different—"

Scipio slammed the lid of the chest shut, silencing Laelius, who expected Scipio to turn, furious and argumentative or grandiose and hopeful. But Scipio did not turn at all. He stood with his hands gripping the lid of the chest. Laelius watched his shoulders heave a sigh, deflating the general like a great gladiator who had finally been bested in the arena.

"You are right," he finally said, still refusing to turn to Laelius. "Instruct the men to do as you have said."

~

In a marshy area along the coast, Scipio and his army established Castra Cornelia. The large Roman base lay at the peak of a rocky peninsula that spiraled out into the sea. The steep, stone-brown cliffside plunged into the turbulent tides below while the glittering crystal sea stretched as far as the horizon. The perimeter walls and towers of Castra Cornelia were built quickly, especially for an army exhausted from a siege. But they had regained their faith in their commander and that hope gave them all the energy they needed.

While beautiful, Castra Cornelia's location was far from ideal. With the open sea at their backs, the army would have to constantly be on the lookout for enemy ships. The base's position on the raised hill cut the army off from the local towns that might lend food or support. Scipio's army did the best it could to fortify Castra Cornelia with little supplies. A small fleet from Sicily and Sardinia replenished many of the army's supplies, which gave rise to an ecstatic celebration among the men. However, with the oncoming winter storms, these supplies from their allies across the sea would have to last them until spring. As the days grew shorter, the army beached the fleet on the sandy shore. The last communication that Scipio received from Rome was a renewal of his command *donec debellatum foret.* The senate had solidified his command "until the war was ended." But thousands of miles away from the city of Rome, across a tempestuous strait, Scipio and his army were on their own.

Two miles to the west stood the impenetrable city and its crumbling tower, reminding Scipio of his failed first strike in Africa. While the icy winter wind blew through the tents and towers of Castra Cornelia, Laelius observed Scipio gazing down upon Utica. His heart felt heavy in his chest as he watched his friend. One day, Laelius finally suggested that the two ride horses down by the shore. Scipio began to lament that he really should be looking over their strategy, but with winter having just begun, there was plenty of time to strategize later.

The sea was moody and turbulent in the silver surf. The sun broke through great gray clouds that grumbled off into the horizon. Laelius waited anxiously for his friend, who seemed hesitant to come in the first place. Perhaps Laelius had waited too long to reach out. Perhaps their hearts had changed too much.

His horse pawed at the sand impatiently, and Laelius patted his neck. "He'll be here."

Sure enough, Scipio appeared at the top of the beach on horseback and rode down to Laelius. "Shall we?" he asked.

"After you, General."

Scipio cocked his eyebrow. "You're not going to let me win that easily, are you?"

With that, he kicked the horse and they sped down the beach. Laelius laughed, egged his own horse on, and within seconds, he had caught up with Scipio. The two experienced horsemen raced side by side on the beach, just as they used to years before when the war was so new in their eyes and home was so much nearer. The friends rode and laughed, splashing in the surf and kicking up the sand like boys, until the sky burned orange with the setting sun. Then the two men dismounted their horses and stared off into the horizon, watching the sun sink lower in the sky. Laelius felt Scipio's tense presence beside him. He knew that something was on his friend's mind and worried that he would be too proud to say it. Laelius had brought them here to the precipice of a stormy sea with the end of the world ahead of them, but Scipio had to make the final leap between them.

Finally, Scipio said, "I am afraid. This war makes me so

afraid. I have lost so much and still there is so much at stake—my family, my legacy, my men, my home and my children's home, and you—"

Laelius turned to see Scipio looking directly at him with the clearest, most sincere eyes he had ever seen.

"Your friendship means more than anything to me, Laelius. I have been so afraid of betrayal, of trusting too much like my father and uncle, that I fear I have lost your friendship. I have shut myself off, refused to trust in our love for one another, to protect myself, but instead, all I have done is cause you to drift away from me. I can never forgive myself for doing that to you."

There was quiet between them, except for the ocean waves gently lapping at the shore.

"When we met," Laelius said, "do you remember what you told me?"

"I asked you to ride with me—"

"Into the sun," Laelius finished. "I always will, my friend."

When Scipio and Laelius returned, they were surprised to find a cloaked figure waiting in Scipio's quarters.

"Who are you?" Scipio immediately demanded, his hand dashing to the hilt of his sword.

The figure floating just above the ground in a gray cloak turned to Scipio and took down his hood.

"Kybe?" Scipio asked.

"It is wonderful to see you again," the gallus laughed, smiling at the general.

"How did you get here? No one can cross *mare nostrum* with these storms."

"It is as I told you," Kybe said simply. "Magna Mater's

influence extends beyond what you might understand." The priest gave Scipio a friendly pat on the shoulder.

"I thought you said you couldn't leave the Galli."

Kybe nodded. "My vocation is to serve Magna Mater, wherever she resides and under whatever name."

"You were in Locri," Laelius remembered suddenly.

"Where the worshippers of Proserpina reside," Kybe added, "just as the people of these villages worship their own goddesses. Some might call these goddesses 'lesser,' but in their true names and truest forms, they are eons older than the Olympians. They come from an age before mare nostrum was split. To serve Magna Mater, I must help unify the sea once more. The Oracle at Delphi bade that Magna Mater reside in Rome, and so Rome must rule the sea."

"We are glad that you came," Scipio told Kybe.

"I must return to Rome soon, but you seemed in need of help in Locri. Now, I am glad to find you in much better spirits," Kybe said. "Even so, perhaps I can contribute to your cause with a bit of information." He gestured southwest, in the direction of the field where the Carthaginians had set up camp. "The goddess worshippers who reside in the town over there informed me that the army decided to build their tents out of reeds and wood without any earth. They warned the soldiers that doing so would have catastrophic effects should one misplaced thunderbolt ignite the field, but most soldiers dismiss the advice of those of us who worship 'lesser goddesses.'"

Kybe gave Scipio a knowing look. "The winter is receding. Spring buds will soon break through the thawing soil. Good luck on your mission, general. May all the gods look favorably upon you."

Scipio nodded and, alongside Laelius, watched the priest glide out of the tent and off to the south. Scipio gazed after Kybe for a few moments before turning to Laelius. They had planning to do.

The last, quiet days of winter bloomed into a rainy spring. Mist hung in the air as Scipio and his men made their way toward Hasdrubal and Syphax's camp. The clouds totally blocked out the moon and stars, ensuring a complete cover of darkness. Silent as the night, Scipio's men spread themselves throughout the enemy camp at the critical points that Scipio and Laelius had outlined. Laelius worried that the moisture in the air would prevent the tents from catching, but when he touched them, the wood felt dry as a bone. Scipio gave a signal by igniting the first spark, and the rest of the men began sparking their flints.

The fire was immense. From a safe distance, Scipio and his men watched the inferno billow up into the sky. The dark night became as bright as day. The camp erupted into chaos as the Carthaginian and Numidian soldiers ran from their tents. Then Scipio gave the second order, and Massinissa's men rode in. The valiant Numidian cavalry captured as many of Syphax and Hasdrubal's men as they could while cutting down and scattering the rest. Scipio and his men joined in the fray as well. The Carthaginians were too panicked and unprepared to mobilize and put up any kind of a fight. They had been caught completely by surprise. By morning light, Syphax and Hasdrubal had escaped, but the rest of the Carthaginian army had been scattered, captured, or felled under a Roman sword.

As the fires died into black smoke that danced in the

morning light, Scipio announced to his generals back at Castra Cornelia that it was time to move.

"Fortuna and Nike have blessed us with a victory," he said. "The winter has passed. Now it is time we concentrate our forces back to the city of Utica."

After the burning of the camps, Carthage was thrown into a panic. Reports reached Scipio's army that included rumors of the Carthaginian Senate desiring to sue for peace, recall Hannibal from Europe, or fight the Romans until the bloody end. Regardless of what the reports said, it was clear that Scipio's presence was disturbing the leaders in Carthage. The Carthaginians could no longer hope to simply bleed the Romans' resources through Utica or strike them from sea. Their army was too diminished now to successfully corner the Romans into the coast. Even more dangerous to the Carthaginians' control over the area was that local villages had begun to side with Scipio. Whether it was distaste for Carthaginian rule, a long-kept allegiance to Massinissa's father, or Scipio's gravitas, the Romans had won the hearts of the people. It was Carthage's move now. In the meantime, Scipio returned to the siege of the impenetrable walled city with renewed vigor. Victory and springtime had renewed his hope for bringing the tower once again into Roman hands.

One month after the burning of the camps, Scipio received intel that Syphax and Hasdrubal had been rallying troops across the region and were planning to meet in the great plain of Campi Magni. Additionally, the Carthaginian Senate had given Hasdrubal four thousand new mercenary troops.

"The fires depleted their troops at the time," Laelius told Scipio, "but if they combine their forces at Campi Magni, they will have a larger army than ever before. Carthage is becoming desperate. They're throwing every last man at us."

"One last battle then," Scipio mused. "One last battle and Carthage's army will be broken."

Scipio left half of the army at Utica to continue the siege, a decision that worried Laelius. If Scipio's army arrived at Campi Magni after the Carthaginians had already combined their forces, a halved army would not stand a chance. What was more, splitting the rations between the two armies would weaken their advance. If Hasdrubal chose to delay battle, then Scipio's men could starve. However, Scipio assured Laelius that the army would move swiftly, and that deserting Utica would do worse to their prospects than taking a fraction of Rome's forces to Campi Magni. He still fervently believed in the siege. Besides, splitting the army would have the added benefit of confounding Carthaginian scouts trying to determine the army's whereabouts.

It took only a few days for Scipio's army to arrive at the plains of Campi Magni. The sky stretched far and wide above the expanse, making Laelius feel as if the fields and the heavens could go on forever in parallel. Young spring grass sprouted up through the soil. In the distance, he could just see the city of Tunis between the plains and Carthage.

When the army arrived at Campi Magni, all were relieved to find that Syphax was not there. However, the Numidian ruler's absence did not make the four thousand Celtic and Iberian mercenaries any less intimidating. As Scipio's men set up their camp, the messenger that the commander had sent ahead confirmed that Hasdrubal would accept the fight. The two armies would battle at dawn.

As the sun began to peek over the horizon and the dew on the grass blades just began to disappear, the cry for battle was sung. Though they stood against the Romans with a larger, highly experienced army, the Carthaginian forces were immediately overwhelmed. Scipio had trained his men to be efficient and quick, using innovative tactics that Hasdrubal had never encountered before. By midday, Rome had won the battle and Hasdrubal had vacated.

"Hasdrubal has once again given up the struggle and fled. He is no favorite of Mars and infamous for his recurrent flights," Scipio announced to his men. "Carthage's army is no more. Hasdrubal will have nowhere to run to except back to the city of Carthage. When he gets there, the city will be in Roman hands."

His men cheered as Scipio stepped away and headed back to his tent in the Roman camp. Laelius and Massinissa met him there. Soon after they all arrived, Cato also entered the tent.

"So, do we return to Utica now?" Laelius asked.

"Cato will return to Utica and protect our men as the siege continues," Scipio said. "We may have defeated Carthage's army, but as soon as they catch wind of Hasdrubal's defeat, they will send their navy to attack us back at Utica. Cato will need to fight them off at sea." He glanced at Cato, who nodded solemnly. "Meanwhile," Scipio said to Laelius, "you and Massinissa must find Syphax. I suspect that with the tide turning away from Carthage's favor, his priorities will be shifting once again. If he does continue to recruit an army, it will be for his own protection and not on behalf of the Carthaginians."

"And where will you go then?" Laelius asked.

"I will ready our men here to walk through the gates of Carthage from the most strategic spot possible," Scipio said simply and gestured to the distant shadow of Tunis.

Chapter Eighteen

A LUCKY ARROW—203 B.C.

Fifteen days after Hasdrubal's defeat, Laelius and Massinissa arrived in Numidia. As they passed between the Numidian towns, they were greeted by cheers and celebration. For the first time, Laelius's eyes were opened to the poverty of the average townspeople. Victims of Syphax's opulence and greed, the Numidians had suffered greatly, stripped of their crops, land, and minerals. Families had been torn apart to provide Syphax with soldiers and slaves. As Massinissa and Laelius traveled from town to town in pursuit of the fleeing king, they listened to the people's heartbreaking stories.

Seeing the plight of the Numidians under Syphax's rule spurred Laelius to recall his own childhood on the farm. He had been so resentful of the Roman nobility and the shamelessness of the sons of the great houses when he was young, but he saw now that he had not endured even half of what these children had. Yet these people were still filled with such joy and gratitude. They had not allowed Syphax's cruelty to break them. Their hope and faith in the Romans gave the two generals strength as they continued their search.

Dining with a Galla, patriarch of one of the villages, Laelius and Massinissa were assured that Syphax would soon be caught.

"He has no more friends in this region," the Galla said, "and when he ruled over us, he made sure that we all would know his face. He may try to build an army to defend himself, but it will be an untrained army of idiots and traitors. Your presence in Numidia will give the other towns hope, as you have given us, and soon all those who once feared and bowed to Syphax will turn to you. He will never see his capital of Cirta again."

After their meal, Massinissa and the Galla spoke at length in a tongue that Laelius did not understand. When Massinissa returned to the generals' lodging for the night, Laelius inquired what the man had asked.

"He wanted to know what I will do when Syphax is captured," Massinissa said.

"You mean, will you return here to take up your father's throne or will you remain with Rome?" Laelius asked.

Massinissa nodded.

Laelius studied him. "And what will you do?"

Massinissa looked up at the bright moon. "I have fought for years to regain what Syphax took from my father, from my family, from me. I believe in Scipio. I am loyal to him. But this is my home. I must return to protect it."

Laelius nodded and smiled at the prince.

The next day, Syphax emerged. He had built up a decent-sized army over the past weeks, one that could certainly face the modest search party that Massinissa and Laelius had brought with them. Laelius hoped that the old man had been right about the men being only traitors and idiots, or else Fortuna would have to smile upon them.

Massinissa called for one of his men to hand him his bow and quiver. Then, in a great, bellowing voice that echoed across the field in which they had found the disgraced king, Massinissa demanded that Syphax surrender.

"Surrender?" Syphax laughed. "A king will not surrender to an orphaned brat and a farm boy!"

Then he gave a great cry, and the battle began.

Laelius drew his sword and cut down one of Syphax's men who had charged at him. Experienced or not, these men were willing to die to see Syphax return to Cirta a free man. Laelius sliced at two more soldiers before, out of the corner of his eye, he saw Syphax himself charge at him. Laelius quickly whipped around, fearing that he wouldn't have time to raise his sword. Suddenly, a lucky arrow hit the flank of Syphax's horse, toppling the king to the ground. Laelius was on him momentarily, trapping Syphax's throat between the ground and his blade. Seeing this, those of Syphax's men who had not already been felled by Massinissa's experienced riders ran off. The battle was over. Laelius looked up gratefully at Massinissa, who held his bow proudly in his hand.

The gates of Cirta opened, permitting Laelius and Massinissa to enter. The people of Cirta watched with shocked expressions as the king who had adorned himself in gold and riches was led, bound, to the capitol building. Before they had even reached the steps, the other nobles had surrendered and began to pledge themselves to Rome. Once the details of the surrender were finalized and Syphax was taken away to be imprisoned under Massinissa's guard, Laelius turned to Massinissa.

"You'll stay, then? To take your father's throne?" he asked.

"There are still those who contest my rule," Massinissa replied. "The fight is not over for either of us, my friend, but I am afraid this is where we part."

"You will be a great king, Massinissa."

"Thank you for helping me apprehend the man who took so much from me."

"You aren't the only one," Laelius said, thinking back to all the Numidian people they had spoken to over the past weeks.

"We have helped many people," Massinissa agreed. "You are a good man, Laelius, and a great horseman. I hope to meet you again soon."

Syphax's defeat shocked the Carthaginian Senate into crisis. When Laelius arrived at Tunis, which had quickly fallen to Scipio after the battle of Campi Magni, Scipio received word that a delegation from Carthage would arrive soon. While Laelius and Massinissa had been in Numidia, Cato had valiantly defended the siege of Utica from a Carthaginian naval onslaught. With Tunis in Roman control, Scipio finally gave up on the siege of the Tower City. The troops that had been left at Utica all came to Tunis, and just a few miles away from Carthage itself, Scipio began the final strategy for attacking the city.

However, Laelius and Massinissa's capture of Syphax pushed the Carthaginians over the edge. A few days after their arrival was announced, the Carthaginian delegation showed up at the gates of Tunis. Laelius, sitting across from the Carthaginians at the negotiation table with Scipio and his other top generals, could tell that while the Carthaginians maintained a façade of strength and nobility, they were afraid of Scipio.

"Carthage is prepared," the leader of the delegation announced to the room, "to surrender all Roman prisoners under Carthaginian control; evacuate our forces from Italy, Gaul, and all the islands between the Italian and African shores; provide twice the customary payment and provisions; and—finally—sign an official treaty between Rome and Carthage, ending this horrific war once and for all."

Scipio stood with power and dignity to face the delegation. A few of the Carthaginians flinched anxiously at his movement, but then relaxed.

"Thank you for your generosity," Scipio said. "If you please, I would like to discuss your proposal with my generals."

The delegation nodded and quickly filed out of the room.

Cato immediately stood as soon as they exited. "We cannot accept this deal, General. It may seem overly generous now, but the Carthaginians are smart. They know that this is their only chance of surviving this war now. With Carthage's fleet, their allies, and most of their fighting forces on land destroyed, we could easily storm and level their city. They realize that, but what they do not realize is how much Rome has suffered. They do not realize how much these men, who have fought and crossed a sea away from their motherland and watched their brothers die, want to see their city reduced to rubble. *They* invaded Italian soil. *They* committed the first act of violence and began this whole war. For that, they must pay. As long as we can, we should fight on."

There was a murmur of agreement among a few of the other generals.

Scipio's eyes grew sad. He sighed and looked to Laelius. "What do you think I should do, my friend?"

Laelius was taken aback. Never had Scipio asked him for his advice so directly above his other generals.

He thought for a while, and finally told his friend, "You are our commander. Whatever you believe we should do is correct. You brought us this far and you can bring us back to Rome."

Then it was Scipio's turn to think, and he thought for a great while. "We did not come here to destroy Carthage. We came to limit its power in order to protect the Republic. We have the opportunity to do so without losing any more Roman lives."

"These men would gladly lose their lives for you!" Cato exclaimed, frustrated. "They want to fight!"

"Do you not think I would be happy to see the walls of Carthage crumble, after everything this war has taken from me and my men and my country?" Scipio snapped back. "Rome has suffered, but must she create more suffering? This mission was never about revenge. It has always been for—I have always fought for—the preservation of the Republic!"

Cato was quiet. Scipio dismissed the generals, saying he had made his decision. But Laelius could see that his friend was conflicted.

When the others had left, Laelius told him, "This is the right decision, Scipio. With Rome supporting Massinissa, Carthage's power will forever be limited, and Hannibal would no longer threaten Rome. He will finally be forced to withdraw. Sixteen years of war will be ended."

Scipio nodded slowly. "Yes . . . but after everything that has happened, knowing that I will never see the city of Carthage burn feels . . . ." He trailed off into his thoughts.

Laelius saw Scipio's pained expression. "Make the diplomatic decision," he said. "It's what your father would have wanted."

Over the next few days, Scipio negotiated terms of

surrender with the delegates from Carthage. Through his consultations with Laelius and those of Massinissa's men who had remained with Scipio, the commander expertly designed terms that would limit Carthage to a regional African power. Never again would a general like Hannibal be permitted to cross onto Italian soil. Carthage quickly accepted Scipio's terms and the senate dispatched a delegation to Rome to formally sign an armistice between the two powers.

Laelius came upon Scipio standing in his quarters in the tower of the Tunisian capital and watched the delegation sail away from Carthage toward his mother country.

"The men are celebrating," Laelius told him. "You should join them. You are their commander."

Scipio turned to Laelius, who could see that Scipio had become teary-eyed. "I feel something that I have never felt my entire life," Scipio said. "Do you feel it, too?"

Laelius nodded. "Yes," he said. "It's peace."

Chapter Nineteen

PEACE BROKEN—203 B.C.

Five months after Carthage representatives first arrived in Rome and attempted to negotiate peace, Hannibal had still refused to leave Italian soil. According to the Carthaginian Senate, he had gone rogue and broken off most communication with the city. In addition, General Mago remained in southern Italy despite being ordered to withdraw along with the rest of the Carthaginian forces based in Europe. The Romans theorized that because of their historical connection, Hannibal was influencing Mago to maintain control over the south so that he could still threaten Rome with a clear protectorate back to Carthage through the south if he needed it.

Hannibal's refusal to cooperate with the armistice was straining the already tenuous relationship between Carthage and Rome as they continued to negotiate a peaceful coexistence. The Carthaginian position was compromised for as long as their top generals remained on Italian soil. Until Hannibal withdrew, Rome would see them as either untrustworthy or too weak to leash their wild dog, both of which would lead to deadly consequences for the African city. Rome, on the other hand, feared that they had backed a beast into a corner. Any move in the wrong direction could mean an attack on the city of Rome itself, which was the last thing that Scipio wanted. All the while, Scipio's enemies in the Roman Senate, who had begrudgingly watched parades in the streets celebrating the great commander after the delegation had arrived in Rome, began to throw blame on Scipio. With peace still only just out of reach, they continued to denounce Scipio's African campaign as a waste of time and Scipio as a weak leader who should have simply leveled Carthage when he had the chance. Fabius the Younger was loudest of all in these accusers. As the end of summer neared, the previous spring's celebrations of peace slipped further and further into memory.

In the meantime, Scipio had established a permanent base in Utica. Carthage had agreed to help Scipio establish his headquarters in the historically Roman settlement as part of their negotiations. It provided them the additional benefit of moving Scipio out of Tunis and thus further away from Carthage itself. Nowhere was the peaceful coexistence of Carthage and Rome tenser than in Africa. Both the Romans and Carthaginians were uncomfortable being in close proximity and neither trusted the other to extend an olive branch beyond what was put forth in the armistice.

The general anxiety and paranoia led to unrest and criticism from Scipio's generals. Cato and those who had implored Scipio to strike down Carthage after the first negotiation acted coldly toward Scipio when they passed him on the streets of Utica. Though no one would go so far as to say that Scipio's diplomacy had failed, disappointment and sadness lay beneath their resentment. They had all so fervently wished for respite from the war.

Scipio, yet again showing his grandiosity and greatness as their commander, expertly navigated criticism from his generals and terse interactions with the Carthaginian delegations that the city would send to Utica to carry out the details of the armistice. However, Laelius could see that the prolonged unsettled peace was weighing on Scipio as well. Every day, Scipio received news of Massinissa's struggles in Numidia against Syphax's followers and other Numidian patriarchs who refused to acknowledge the banished prince's claim to the throne. Syphax's son, Vermina, had built up a small force of his own and was leading a campaign against Massinissa to resurrect his father's name. Scipio began to receive intelligence that some parties within the Carthaginian Senate were lobbying to break the armistice and restart the war. Nothing more than whispered conversations suggested such things, but as time went on, the war party appeared to be gaining more and more political sway within the senate. The people of Carthage were feeding off Hannibal's refusal to concede to the peace terms. Even across the sea, the legendary general's influence motivated his people. As more time passed, the peace that Scipio's men had celebrated only months earlier withered.

Scipio used the peacetime, tenuous though it was, as an opportunity to resupply the army. With a permanent base at Utica, Scipio's men could finally stop supplying themselves from mobile rations and could set up more substantial food stores and weaponries. Scipio sent a request to Rome for more rations, and received a message that two large resupply ship convoys would be headed their way. He instructed his men to ready themselves for the arrival of these supplies, lifting their spirits for a moment during a tense period. When the first convoy of one hundred transports arrived, escorted by twenty Roman warships, the entirety of Utica rejoiced and celebrated late into the night.

But the second ship never arrived. Then Scipio began receiving reports of a storm that had scattered the convoy off the promontory of Apollo. Most of the convoy's warship escort had safely reached the shore, but the supply transports had been shipwrecked on an island called Aegimurus, just off the coast of Carthage. The island was so close that its center could be seen from the city. When scouts from the warships attempted to rescue the beached transports, Carthaginian ships beat them to the island and emptied the Roman supplies.

Then the Carthaginians became more aggressive. The smaller, lightly protected transports that regularly sailed with more minimal supplies between Sardinia and Utica began to be intercepted by Carthaginian ships. The Carthaginian Senate claimed that these were stolen ships piloted by rogue pirates, but Scipio was skeptical. His generals demanded that Scipio respond aggressively toward Carthage, but Scipio had other plans.

One evening, the week after the second transport was discovered empty, Laelius was summoned to Scipio's chambers. When he entered the room, he found Scipio and a small group of soldiers dressed in cloaks similar to the one that Massinissa had worn when Laelius had first met him. Scipio offered Laelius a cloak. Laelius looked at the commander quizzically.

"We are taking a brief journey," Scipio said. "If the Carthaginians continue to refuse to respond to reasonable correspondence, perhaps they will respond to an appearance. We can't be sure now whether Carthage will be hostile or if they will to continue to deceive us, so we will surprise them with a diplomatic visit."

"You're sneaking into the city? To speak with the senate?"

Scipio nodded and offered Laelius the cloak again. "We are."

The city of Carthage looked and felt more like Rome than Laelius had expected. Had he not known where the convoy was headed, he might have mistaken the crowded apartments and busy marketplace for the familiar streets of Rome. As they approached the Carthaginian Senate forum, Laelius thought back to the distant memories he held dear of his own country. He wondered when he would once again walk the stone streets of his beloved city.

Suddenly, Laelius heard a shout. Scipio turned and the two could see a merchant angrily pointing at Scipio. They had been spotted. A crowd formed around the Romans and Scipio drew his sword in preparation. But as quickly as the crowd had formed, they were scattered by a group of Carthaginian soldiers led by a trio of senators. Scipio and Laelius were quickly escorted into the senate chambers. It was clear that the townspeople of Carthage had no desire for diplomacy toward the Romans.

Upon entering the chamber and seeing the other Carthaginian senators, Scipio revealed himself.

"General Scipio," one of the senators said, "we were not expecting to see you here. We would have arranged a convoy—"

"I am here to speak to the Roman convoys," Scipio interrupted, "who have been robbed and harassed for the past week."

"We are deeply apologetic," another senator spoke, "but those rogue ships, they are out of our hands."

Something in his tone told Laelius that what the senator had spoken was untrue.

Scipio heard it as well and was a great deal more impatient. "If our supply ships continue to be beached by Carthaginian boats, our truce will be broken. This is all I have come to tell you. My presence here is to emphasize the gravity of that situation should it occur—and I wanted to look in the eyes the men who might doom their country should they continue behaving in such a manner."

The senators clearly did not appreciate Scipio's final statement, but Laelius could also see that they were terrified of the general.

The first senator who had spoken nodded his head and stood humbly. "General Scipio, please return to Utica. We can provide an escort to ensure that you will return to the city safely."

As they left the chamber, escorted by three gruff-looking Carthaginian soldiers, Scipio turned to Laelius and whispered, "Den of snakes! Hope for peace is lost. They want war, but they want to act as if our truce means something to them long enough for them to prepare a strike against us."

Laelius shot Scipio a look, confirming that he had come to the same conclusion.

Back on the ship, Scipio sensed heightened tension as they began their departure. Scipio's ship made it safely out of the harbor, escorted by the Carthaginian warships just as the senators had promised. However, upon exiting the Macar River, which fed into the sea, Scipio suddenly lost sight of the escort. Slowly, the other Romans on the ship began to realize what was happening. They were to sail back alone, their identities now exposed.

After a few hours, Utica was in sight. Laelius could see Scipio visibly relax, though a shadow remained over his face. Without the promise of peace, war was once again upon them, only now Scipio would have to act. If Carthage continued to bleed Rome's supplies through "rebel" ships, then Scipio would have to make the first major demonstration, breaking the peace treaty that he himself had negotiated. But Laelius saw that he was determined. The other generals had been right all along. Something had to be done.

Suddenly, Laelius heard a shout from one of the sailors. He and Scipio turned to find that three Carthaginian ships had appeared out of nowhere and were barreling down on the Romans. With the shore in sight, the captain tried to catch the wind and speed the ship toward the beach, but the Carthaginian ships quickly surrounded them. Still, Scipio's captain whipped around the warships, narrowly avoiding one collision after another. His excellent steering gave those at Utica time to spot the chase, and in no time, more Roman warships had been dispatched from the shore. After an hour of dodging attack, Scipio's ship was saved by the Roman naval fleet, which successfully fought away the Carthaginian ships. When they landed back on shore safely, Laelius gratefully fell to the sand and breathed deeply. Never had he been so relieved to clutch sand in his fists.

Once they were back in Utica, Scipio received an important message: Mago had just landed in Africa and Hannibal himself was set to land at Hadrumetum any day. His generals asked Scipio what they should do next.

"The peace is broken," Scipio told them. "Ready the men for battle."

Chapter Twenty

ZAMA—202 B.C.

After Hannibal successfully landed his army at Hadrumetum, most Roman and Carthaginian diplomats alike expected the infamous general to immediately engage Scipio. Yet, weeks after Hannibal had returned to North Africa, he had refused to even acknowledge Scipio's presence. The Roman stronghold in Utica remained poised should they spot Hannibal's army on the horizon, but Hannibal left them undisturbed. Like an ever-tensed muscle, the army began to grow tired and anxious as time went on. It seemed as if Hannibal would not even dignify the Romans with a fight.

Frustrated, Scipio began a campaign in the area surrounding Utica, attacking towns that had remained loyal to Carthage. He hoped that this would draw Hannibal's army out into the field. Scipio knew that Hannibal's army was too powerful and too well fortified to simply attack, so they would have to meet on the battlefield. He and Laelius worked from dusk until dawn, strategizing new ways that they could spur the Carthaginian general into action. Scipio became increasingly more desperate to incite Hannibal as his men drew further away from the base at Utica and away from the safety of immediate reinforcements from the city should his men be attacked.

Finally, Scipio received word from a general on the outskirts of the campaign that Hannibal's army was marching out of Hadrumetum and appeared to be heading inland. Only a few hours later, one of Massinissa's men arrived at Utica with a message from his commander. The army of Vermina, Syphax's son, had grown exponentially. Hannibal's return to Africa had brought out more supporters of Syphax than Massinissa had thought still existed, and they had all joined Vermina's army. Vermina was on his way to join forces with Hannibal now. With Vermina's forces, the garrison that had sailed with Hannibal from Italy would explode in size and totally outnumber Scipio's army, eliminating any chance of Scipio defeating Hannibal in battle.

"We cannot let Vermina reach Hannibal," Scipio told Laelius. "We must rejoin Massinissa's men and attack Hannibal's army before they rendezvous."

"Zama," Laelius said, pointing to the region on Scipio's map. "It's right in Vermina's path, and our legions should be able to arrive there long before he or Hannibal does. It's an ideal spot to engage Hannibal, and we will have had enough time to establish a fortified camp by the time that Hannibal comes upon us."

"Zama it is," Scipio confirmed.

As the Roman legions approached Zama, Laelius was shocked to find that his calculations had been incorrect. In the distance, Laelius and Scipio could see the tops of Carthaginian tents.

Hannibal was already there. Catching a glimpse of the infamous general's camp, the men began to murmur behind Scipio and Laelius. Scipio directed them to shift their course, and the army continued marching to an open field just outside of Zama.

"It's as if he expected us to meet him here," Scipio whispered to Laelius, who nodded.

Thankfully, there was no way that Vermina had arrived yet with his forces, or else all hope would be lost. The Roman army set up their camp as the sun began to set. Hannibal's camp sat ominously in the distance.

That evening, as Scipio and Laelius were discussing the plan for the following morning, a group of scouts entered the commander's tent.

"General," said a young man who could not have been older than sixteen, "there is a group of Carthaginian spies surveying the camp. What should we do when we capture them?"

"Let them spy," Scipio told them. "We have nothing to hide."

The scouts looked at one another confused, but rather than question orders, they left the tent.

"What are you thinking?" Laelius asked Scipio. By now, he knew when his friend had a plan.

Scipio looked at Laelius as he often had when he harbored a secret agenda that he did not trust anyone with knowing.

"The cavalry," Scipio told him. "Massinissa's men haven't arrived yet, and if Hannibal thinks that this is the extent of our forces, he will see that we have a weak cavalry. When Massinissa arrives, that could tip the scale."

There was a ruckus outside of the tent.

"The spies must have caught the attention of others," Laelius guessed.

Scipio stood and walked out, closely followed by Laelius. They saw a scrawny Carthaginian youth standing in the center of the camp, surrounded by Scipio's soldiers. He looked proud despite his stature and stood his ground. The Roman soldiers regarded him like a young venomous snake.

The youth's gaze shifted to Scipio. "General Scipio, I have a message from General Hannibal Barca. He requests a peaceful rendezvous away from the camps at Naragara, just west of here. He wishes to meet face-to-face with the greatest Roman general of all time."

The message came as a shock to everyone. After weeks of ignoring Scipio, Hannibal now wanted to meet with him? Scipio had expected anything but this. He looked to Laelius, who had the same reaction of surprise, then turned back to the youth.

"Tell General Hannibal that I accept his request."

The following evening, Scipio and a small protectorate traveled west to Naragara toward their intended meeting spot near the mountains. Scipio was quiet throughout the journey and deep in thought. Laelius wondered what his friend might be thinking as he himself tried to deduce the true purpose of this meeting. The sun was low when they arrived at the location for the rendezvous. The sky began to glow, and the mountains and the fields took on a golden quality. Some called this the golden hour, the short period of time between day and night just before sunset, when all the world basked in the aura of Apollo's chariot.

As the sky faded from gold into a rusty orange, Laelius watched Hannibal's protectorate appear. As he approached, Laelius could see why so many men heeded his command. Hannibal possessed a graciousness and power that Laelius had only seen in the greatest generals, but most of all Scipio. In fact, Hannibal carried himself much like Publius the Elder had, and like Laelius imagined Scipio would in later years. The most striking difference between the two generals was the great black beard that Hannibal proudly displayed.

When the general came before Scipio, he broke into a wide, charismatic smile. "General Scipio," Hannibal said. "I am so glad that I finally have the chance to meet you. I have admired your courage and spirit for years."

Scipio was taken aback, though he tried not to show it. "I was surprised by your request for this meeting, General Hannibal."

"Surprised?" Hannibal chuckled. "Why? Because we are on opposite sides of this war? General," he cooed, his commanding voice now sounding intimate, "you and I are not so different. Had history played out in another way, we could perhaps fight side by side. I can see that you take after your father."

Scipio's jaw tightened. "What do you know of my father?"

"He was a man I admired much as well. He was a brave and intelligent leader. I can only imagine what it must have been like to know him as you did."

"But you did not," Scipio asserted. "You did not know him—not like I did, not like his family did. Had you known him, you would have ended this war when he died." His breath quickened. Laelius watched his friend's face grow red with emotion that he tried not to show.

Hannibal nodded and looked to Scipio with understanding eyes. "I, too, grew up in a family of great military ambition. If I am not mistaken, you and I entered the military at the same age, though I confess that seems a lifetime away for me now. When my father was defeated at the Aegates Islands, I was angry. I felt betrayed. I, too, believed that my father was the best general who had ever been born. My father was not a perfect man, nor a perfect general, but he made me the man I have become and the general I am today. I crossed the sea to resume this war because I was angry and passionate to continue what my father could not."

Hannibal gazed at the horizon. Up close, he appeared older than Laelius had thought, his eyes deep with wisdom but hardened with experience. "I, too, have never known a world without war, General Scipio. Perhaps that is what makes us such good generals. We understand how much is lost in a world at war. Don't you think?"

"Yes," Scipio said softly. He seemed to glean his opponent's wisdom.

"And you and I share a fervent love for our countries, and our patriotism is what brought us across the sea into a strange land. Ours is one story, General Scipio, retold with different names."

Scipio's muscles stiffened. He opened his mouth to reply, but Hannibal cut him off.

"I believe that Rome and Carthage could be the world's two greatest powers," Hannibal said. "If we join together, there is nothing that can stop us."

The quiet of the evening hung in the air. The sky had become deep red like blood.

Scipio looked at the older general. He finally replied, "Carthage has no place on Italian soil. You began this war. Carthage grew beyond its limits and tried to destroy Mother Rome. You and your men have ravaged our country and held our motherland in the grips of fear for too long. You may be a great general, Hannibal Barca, but Carthage will never stand at Rome's gates again with fire or friendship. The day will be won on the battlefield, and then we will have peace."

"So be it," said Hannibal, who then graciously departed with his protectorate before Scipio could say anything more.

Scipio was again quiet as they traveled back to the Roman camp. But this time it was a silence heavy with doubt. When they returned, Scipio sat solemnly, looking at his father's maps lit by the firelight.

Laelius came to check on him. "What is it, my friend?"

"What if what he said is true?" Scipio said quietly. "What if Hannibal and I are one story retold with different names?"

Laelius considered this. "Even if that is so," he told his friend, "your intentions have always been valiant. It is as you said: Carthage started this war. To achieve peace for all sides, we must finish it."

Scipio looked at Laelius. His eyes were wide and bright, reflecting the dancing flames. Then he stood and embraced his friend, as if it might be their last night together.

Early the next morning, both armies faced one another on the field of Zama. Thirty thousand Roman infantrymen and one thousand cavalrymen poised to fight to the death against fifteen thousand Iberian and Gaul mercenaries, ten thousand Carthaginian infantrymen, three thousand cavalrymen, and eighty war elephants. At the center of Hannibal's army was the Old Guard, veteran Lucanians and Brutti fighters from the south of Italy who had pledged themselves to Hannibal. They were Hannibal's top fighters, experienced and disciplined, numbering another fifteen thousand. Knowing that Hannibal would bolster the center of his army with the Old Guard, Scipio structured his forces similarly, placing his best fighters at the center. When the sun just peeked above the mountaintops, the battle commenced.

Laelius could never thereafter remember a battle as chaotic as Zama. Battling the Carthaginian forces was like slaying a

Hydra. Every time he swung his sword and cut down an enemy, another enemy replaced him. Men and horses and armor and the sharpest steel crashed down on him like terrifying ocean waves. They crashed above and around him for hours. All he could hear was the irregular, sickening thud of sword on flesh and bone intermingled with painful cries. The battlefield glistened with pools of ruby blood.

Time passed quickly and yet not at all. Laelius tried to remain as close to Scipio as possible, fending off any enterprising Carthaginians who might have wished to cut down the great general. On one of the few occasions he permitted himself to look at the battle beyond as a whole, he saw a group of soldiers take down one of Hannibal's war elephants. The great creature gave a trumpeting scream as it fell. Most of the time, Laelius could not risk taking his gaze away from the field in front of his face. Adrenaline coursed through his body as he swung again and again. Scipio fought off the waves beside him.

Still, Hannibal's men continued to push Scipio's army farther back. Hannibal and the Old Guard, clearly the most skilled soldiers in a highly skilled and vicious army, overtook Scipio's front lines immediately. As the day went on, Hannibal's core drilled into the center of Scipio's army, slaughtering all in their path. The Old Guard drew close enough that Laelius could see the glint of their swords in the distance. The stench of death surrounded them. Dark shadows passed over the sun, causing Laelius to look up. Vultures soared high above their heads expectantly.

Then came a sound that Laelius would never forget. When Scipio's forces had been overwhelmed and pushed backward almost irreparably, Laelius heard a soft thunder beneath his feet growing louder and louder, coming from the west. Every soldier appeared to pause for a moment, sensing the thunder as well. It was the thunder of horse hooves. Laelius looked at the horizon, and as if sent by the gods themselves, Massinissa appeared. He and his riders sped into the maelstrom with their famed intensity.

The addition of Massinissa's cavalry overturned all of Hannibal's planning, bewildering the Carthaginian army and turning the tide of the fight in the Romans' favor. With Massinissa upon Hannibal's army, Scipio's army surged forward with new confidence.

Laelius dove bravely into the waves of men. Like valiant dolphins, he and Scipio careened through the Carthaginian forces. Their swords were invincible; their power, unmatched. For a minute, Laelius felt propelled by Mercury's winged sandals, strengthened by the might of Mars, and wielding Zeus's famous thunderbolt.

Then, as if Laelius had been thrust forward in time, all of a sudden the battle was finished. The sun glinted above the horizon. Against all odds, Scipio stood victorious on the battlefield. Rome had won.

When the prisoners, the wounded, and the dead had been accounted for, Scipio's men found that Hannibal had escaped. Immediately, a search party was sent after the Carthaginian general.

"Do not worry," Scipio reassured his generals. "He is defeated. He has no more friends here. Once he is apprehended, he will be tried before the senate in Rome."

He smiled, his expression a mix of pride and relief. The war was finally over.

That evening, Scipio's men celebrated the victory while the generals began plans to return to Italy. All the men spoke of their wives, children, families, and friends that they would soon see once again. They toasted to those souls who had died so valiantly on the field. They started to make lists of all the families and widows with whom they would mourn and would protect as if they were the men's own wives and families. They cried and laughed, drank and danced, and made tributes to Fortuna and Mars and Jupiter. Most of all, they praised their commander, who had led them to this victorious day.

Laelius finally found Scipio alone for a moment. He was in his tent, packing up the maps that his father had passed down to him.

"Publius Scipio the Elder. He is the one they should be thanking," Scipio muttered to himself. "All I did was continue his legacy, walk in his footsteps."

Laelius shook his head. "You are your own man, my friend. You led us here."

"By his example."

"But with your own greatness."

Scipio smiled at the thought.

Lucius poked his head into the tent. "Brother, a message from Rome! They congratulate you on your victory!" He handed the message to Scipio, who read it over.

Scipio's brow furrowed. "What is this?" he asked, pointing to the message's address.

"Hadn't you heard?" Lucius laughed. "They've begun to call you that in the city now—endearingly. I heard it was Aemelia who came up with it to commemorate your accolades and your bravery, not only in Italy, but more importantly, beyond."

The general looked back at the senate's message addressed to "Scipio Africanus."

Epilogue

A NEW ROME—160 B.C.

R*ome is so much hotter than Arcadia*, Polybius thought as he made his way through the crowded street of artisans and fruit vendors. The city of Rome was north of the Greek metropolis, and yet the past few summers had been the hottest that Polybius had ever experienced. Perhaps an explanation lay in the brilliant colors: the dazzling golds, fiery reds, and kingly purples displayed across the great city. Rome was a jewel brighter now than ever. What was once a small principality of enterprising Italian tribes had been forged through decades of war into the golden beacon of civilization through which Polybius navigated.

Perhaps there was an alternative explanation. Did Polybius feel the heat of Rome's glory through the sweat on his brow or did he miss the cooling breeze of his Greek home? Home, he thought. Every day he missed home. For seven years he had been detained in Rome as a hostage for his father's recklessness with no hope of return in the near future. But Polybius had decided to make the best of his scenario. While other Greek noblemen who suffered a similar fate wasted away in the purposeless opulence of their Roman counterparts' homes, Polybius wanted to do something. He had been a historian back in Arcadia, and his studies of Greek geography and history had inevitably given him a vast knowledge of Rome's. He had made it his mission to continue his work as a historian.

Walking past the carts overflowing with golden wheat, fragrant meats and cheeses, emerald olive oil, and vibrantly dyed fabrics of every color, it was easy to forget that Rome had been enmeshed in two wars not long ago. It was this forgetting during times of plenty that spurred Polybius on his mission. War, he believed, created stories, and it was the role of the historian to seek them out. That was not to say that being a historian was merely a civic duty. In possession of an ever-curious mind, he had always been fascinated with the rise of the greatest city on the Mediterranean. His work as a historian in Arcadia had also taught him that in retellings of the past lay the secrets of the present. The more time that Polybius spent in the archives of the wars that had brought him to Rome as a prisoner, the more hope he had that he might find a way to return home. His hope, as well as his unquenchable curiosity, had brought him to the distinguished house that stood before him.

Gaius Laelius was one of Rome's most prominent figures. A war hero in his own right, Laelius also happened to have been the best friend and right hand of Publius Cornelius Scipio Africanus. Polybius admired no one more than Scipio Africanus. Not only was the man a renowned military figure, but he had a brilliant mind and was a shrewd diplomat as well. After defeating the great Carthaginian general Hannibal Barca, Scipio returned to Rome and was immediately elected *princeps senatus*. His political career brought Rome the prosperousness it enjoyed almost as much as his military career did. Throughout his lifetime, he successfully evaded multiple attempts of his enemies to discredit him, including a political disaster involving his brother, Lucius. He bolstered his son Publius's political career as well.

Interestingly, throughout his life, Scipio defended his old enemy, Hannibal. The two often exchanged correspondence throughout the years following Hannibal's defeat at Zama. After Scipio had retired and slipped out of the public eye, he came to Hannibal's defense when Rome attempted to ruin the aging Carthaginian general after he had been exiled. He was a man of the people and died one of Rome's greatest leaders.

Polybius was shaken from the labyrinth of his mind by the sound of youthful shouting. Two young men—they couldn't be older than fifteen—were sparring in the front yard of the villa between two olive trees. The younger, whom Polybius realized must have been Laelius's son Sapiens, had a striking resemblance to his father. He did not possess the softer features of a Roman nobleman, but instead carried himself with the nimbleness and forcefulness of a cavalryman.

"Young man," Polybius shouted to the two boys, who stopped their sparring and approached him. "Is your father within?"

"He is, with his aunt," the young Sapiens replied. "Are you the man he was expecting?"

"I am. Where might I find him?"

Before the young man could answer, an astonishingly beautiful woman appeared in the front doorway. Wildflowers had been braided into her hair, and her indigo tunic blew lightly in the breeze. In her presence, Polybius no longer saw the entryway to a great house, but instead, the baldachin of a queen's throne. When her eyes fell upon him, Polybius felt the appraisal of centuries of great Roman women.

"You must be the writer of history," she said in a voice lighter than sea foam. "I am Cornelia."

Polybius approached Scipio Africanus's daughter and took her hand. She smiled.

"It is an honor to meet you, my lady," Polybius said.

"Come," she cooed, gathering her robe. "Let me show you inside."

As she turned, Polybius noticed a small boy clutching her robe in his small tan fist and looking up at him with eyes as large as copper saucers.

"Tiberius, say hello to the man," his mother instructed.

Instead, the boy ran ahead of the two adults and disappeared into another room. Cornelia laughed musically.

"I was sorry to hear of your mother's passing," Polybius said.

Cornelia's bright, joyful eyes took on a sadder shape. "Yes. Many of the women in Rome hoped she might be immortal, but her family knew that she was simply a great woman. But you have come to talk to Laelius about my father."

"Yes. I am hoping to record a history of the Punic Wars."

"You aren't the first. Sempronius came to my father when he was still alive to record his account of the wars, and he declined. Laelius was more receptive and gave his own account, but the past has not changed. Why not simply leave it with Sempronius?"

"I have read Sempronius's history of the Second War, but I believe that there is no better source of truth than the words of those who witnessed the events with their own eyes."

They came to a veranda that led out to a beautifully manicured garden and Cornelia turned to Polybius. "He is much older now than when he was in the war. Even if he is still receptive, he may have forgotten some of the truths that you seek."

"You're protective of him."

"He is like an uncle to me, and now that my father is gone . . . ."

She looked out into the garden. Polybius followed her gaze and was surprised to see the small boy Tiberius in conversation with an older man seated on a stone bench beside a burbling fountain.

"I just mean to warn you that you may not find anything new," she said, and led Polybius out to the old man seated by the fountain.

Laelius saw Cornelia approaching with the young man. He could read the face of someone looking for a good story instantly. He had become accustomed to such an expression long ago.

"What are you thinking, Uncle?" Cornelia asked when she came to the fountain.

"Horses, my dear," Laelius chuckled. "Is there ever anything else?"

Cornelia smiled sweetly. She was an incredibly intelligent young woman. Laelius could see that she and her sons had inherited greatness from her father. His age had given him an understanding of things that he, as a young man, never would have thought he could possess.

"This man would like to talk to you about Father," Cornelia said.

"I am a historian," Polybius began. "I have admired everything that you and Scipio Africanus have done for this country—"

"I will tell you everything that you would like to know,"

Laelius cut him off. "But not now. I am tired. Come back tomorrow morning. Early."

The Greek man thanked him immensely. Cornelia told him that she would escort him out. Before they walked off, she turned back to Laelius.

"Can I bring you anything, Uncle?"

"No, my dear. I will rest here for just a moment."

She smiled and walked off with the young man.

Laelius closed his eyes. He felt the sun beat down on his brow. He listened to the fountain as it became waves on the African shore—or perhaps it was Spanish or Sicilian. He heard the soft clomping of horse hooves in sand while he and his old friend raced toward Apollo's chariot. *He caught it,* Laelius thought. *He finally caught it.*

About the Author

Patric Verrone is a writer, theatrical artist and student of the world originally from Los Angeles. He studied psychology with a secondary in studies in women, gender, and sexuality at Harvard University. His plays have been produced and workshopped by the Blank Theater in Los Angeles, the Harvard Playwrights Festival, and The Custom Made Theater in San Francisco. Recently, he has researched under the guidance of Michael Bronski for an upcoming anthology series of collected historical essays. When he isn't writing, Patric loves to take hikes with his dog.

NOW AVAILABLE FROM THE MENTORIS PROJECT

America's Forgotten Founding Father
A Novel Based on the Life of Filippo Mazzei
by Rosanne Welch, PhD

A. P. Giannini—The People's Banker
by Francesca Valente

The Architect Who Changed Our World
A Novel Based on the Life of Andrea Palladio
by Pamela Winfrey

A Boxing Trainer's Journey
A Novel Based on the Life of Angelo Dundee
by Jonathan Brown

Breaking Barriers
A Novel Based on the Life of Laura Bassi
by Jule Selbo

Building Heaven's Ceiling
A Novel Based on the Life of Filippo Brunelleschi
by Joe Cline

Building Wealth
From Shoeshine Boy to Real Estate Magnate
by Robert Barbera

Building Wealth 101
How to Make Your Money Work for You
by Robert Barbera

Christopher Columbus: His Life and Discoveries
by Mario Di Giovanni

Dark Labyrinth
A Novel Based on the Life of Galileo Galilei
by Peter David Myers

Defying Danger
A Novel Based on the Life of Father Matteo Ricci
by Nicole Gregory

The Divine Proportions of Luca Pacioli
A Novel Based on the Life of Luca Pacioli
by W.A.W. Parker

Dreams of Discovery
A Novel Based on the Life of the Explorer John Cabot
by Jule Selbo

The Faithful
A Novel Based on the Life of Giuseppe Verdi
by Collin Mitchell

Fermi's Gifts
A Novel Based on the Life of Enrico Fermi
by Kate Fuglei

First Among Equals
A Novel Based on the Life of Cosimo de' Medici
by Francesco Massaccesi

God's Messenger
A Novel Based on the Life of Mother Frances X. Cabrini
by Nicole Gregory

Grace Notes
A Novel Based on the Life of Henry Mancini
by Stacia Raymond

Harvesting the American Dream
A Novel Based on the Life of Ernest Gallo
by Karen Richardson

Humble Servant of Truth
A Novel Based on the Life of Thomas Aquinas
by Margaret O'Reilly

Leonardo's Secret
A Novel Based on the Life of Leonardo da Vinci
by Peter David Myers

Little by Little We Won
A Novel Based on the Life of Angela Bambace
by Peg A. Lamphier, PhD

The Making of a Prince
A Novel Based on the Life of Niccolò Machiavelli
by Maurizio Marmorstein

A Man of Action Saving Liberty
A Novel Based on the Life of Giuseppe Garibaldi
by Rosanne Welch, PhD

Marconi and His Muses
A Novel Based on the Life of Guglielmo Marconi
by Pamela Winfrey

No Person Above the Law
A Novel Based on the Life of Judge John J. Sirica
by Cynthia Cooper

Relentless Visionary: Alessandro Volta
by Michael Berick

Soldier, Diplomat, Archaeologist
A Novel Based on the Bold Life of Louis Palma di Cesnola
by Peg A. Lamphier, PhD

The Soul of a Child
A Novel Based on the Life of Maria Montessori
by Kate Fuglei

What a Woman Can Do
A Novel Based on the Life of Artemisia Gentileschi
by Peg A. Lamphier, PhD

FUTURE TITLES FROM THE MENTORIS PROJECT

A Biography about Rita Levi-Montalcini
and
Novels Based on the Lives of:
Amerigo Vespucci
Andrea Doria
Antonin Scalia
Antonio Meucci
Buzzie Bavasi
Cesare Beccaria
Father Eusebio Francisco Kino
Federico Fellini
Frank Capra
Guido d'Arezzo
Harry Warren
Leonardo Fibonacci
Maria Gaetana Agnesi
Mario Andretti
Peter Rodino
Pietro Belluschi
Saint Augustine of Hippo
Saint Francis of Assisi
Vince Lombardi

For more information on these titles and
the Mentoris Project, please visit
www.mentorisproject.org

40776370R00154